UNVEILED MYSTERIES

UNVEILED MYSTERIES

BY
GODFRE RAY KING

KALPAZ

First Published in 1934
Indian Reprint in 2017

Published by

Kalpaz Publications
C-30, Satyawati Nagar,
Delhi – 110052
E-mail: kalpaz@hotmail.com
Website: kalpazpublications.com
Ph.: +91-9212142040

Cataloging in Publication Data—DK
Courtesy: D.K. Agencies (P) Ltd. <docinfo@dkagencies.com>

King, Godfreì Ray, 1878-1939, **author.**
Unveiled mysteries / Godfre Ray King.
pages cm
Reprint.
ISBN 9789351286172 (HB)

1. I AM Religious Activity. I. Title.

BP605.I18K57 2017 DDC 299.93 23

DEDICATION

This series of books is dedicated in deepest, Eternal Love and Gratitude to our Beloved Master, Saint Germain, the Great White Brotherhood, the Brotherhood of the Royal Teton, the Brotherhood of Mount Shasta, and those other Ascended Masters whose loving help has been direct and without limit.

Contents

TRIBUTE

The time has arrived, when the Great Wisdom, held and guarded for many centuries in the Far East, is now to come forth in America, at the command of those Great Ascended Masters who direct and protect the evolution of mankind upon this earth.

The Great Ascended Master, Saint Germain, throughout this series of books, is one of those Powerful Emissaries from the Spiritual Hierarchy of Ascended Masters who govern this planet.

He is the same Great Masterful "Presence" who worked at the Court of France previous to and during the French Revolution and whose advice, if it had been heeded, would have saved great suffering. It was because of his Transcendently Divine Power that he was referred to at that time as "Der Wundermann" of Europe. He is indissolubly linked with America past, present, and future for a very important part of his work upon this earth is the purifying, protecting, and illumining of the people of America that she may be the Carrier of the Cup of "Light" to the nations of the earth in the Golden Age that is opening before us.

America's very freedom in the beginning of her existence was due largely to his tireless efforts in protecting and encouraging those responsible for her inception. The drafting of the Declaration of Independence was also a direct result of his help and influence, and it was his love, protection, and guidance which sustained Washington and Lincoln during the darkest hours of their lives.

This Beloved Brother of humanity, who works untiringly for its Light and Freedom, is even now during the present hour in America working in the world of governmental affairs and bringing about certain beneficial changes that will bless her and through her the world. Not for many years ahead, will the people of America and the earth know how much of their good they owe to this Great Ascended Master to whom it is impossible to do full justice, except in deepest love, obedience, and service to the Ideal for which he stands and ceaselessly labors.

This intimate knowledge of his activities in our country makes possible a feeling of close contact and love for him that becomes a living tangible force in the life of the reader.

The radiation of this book is such as can only be given by an Ascended Master who in this case is the Great Beloved "Bearer of the Light," Saint Germain.

GODFRE RAY KING

FOREWORD

It was through Saint Germain's assistance that I was privileged to have the experiences re corded in this series of books, and that permission has been granted for them to be put in a form which can be given to the public. No one can realize, unless he too has had similar assistance, how great and eternal is my love and gratitude to him and those other Ascended Masters, whose assistance I had.

With the exception of Saint Germain, the real names of the Ascended Masters, exact locations, records, and treasure herein described are withheld intentionally at his command, for reasons that are obvious because only by the Service of Love and invitation from the Ascended Masters is the right earned to be with them in visible, tangible, living, breathing bodies. Any other way of approach is bound to meet with disappointment and failure, for the Great "Presence" and Power which has guarded through the centuries, guards them still.

One's own Inner purity, strength, and attainment are the only passports by which one enters into these activities, and association with the Ascended Masters comes about. When an individual, by conscious self-correction of his weaknesses, reaches a certain point, nothing in the universe can keep him from them.

In America is one of the most Ancient Foci of the Great White Brotherhood which has been working for man's freedom since his advent upon this planet. Some of the activities within this retreat are revealed to the reader that he may, if he be ready, make conscious contact, through his own Inner Light, with the Greater Light pouring out through this powerful center of God-radiation, and thereby drink once again at the Fountain of the Ancient Wisdom and carry the Crystal Cup of Peace, Love, and Strength to his weary brothers.

The purpose of putting this book into the hands of the public is to convey to the individual the encouragement and strength that will lift and sustain him through the transition period we are now in, and reveal something of the sane and sound foundation upon which the future of our country and the coming age is this hour being built.

This book is written in the embrace of the majestic, towering presence of Mount Shasta, whose apex is robed forever in that pure, glistening white, the symbol of the "Light of Eternity." Its pages are a record of the way by which

I was brought in touch with the Beloved Master, Saint Germain, and those other Great Ascended Masters who labor ceaselessly to assist the humanity of this earth, as it struggles on the path to Peace, Love, Light, and Everlasting Perfection.

I, whose experience it was, held steadfastly to a great dominant desire from Within to see, to hear, and to know, infallibly, the Truth of Life. I was led step by step to realize and accept the Mighty God "Presence" within my own Being—the "Light that lighteth every man that cometh into the world"—the "Christ." A way to make contact with the Christ—"Light," Its All-Knowing Omnipresence, and Unerring Activity was revealed to me, and I give it to the reader in these pages.

I can record only a part of the events that took place and the instruction I received. One by one, my great desires have been fulfilled because those desires were unselfish. My quest for Truth and Happiness has been long and steady but I have found both, and no human being can take them from me because they are Eternal and come from my own Great God Self.

In presenting this experience, it is with the deepest prayer that the reader may receive the "Light," be blest, and prospered on his way, as he walks the Path of Truth which is the only place where permanent happiness can be found. There, and there only, will the Seeker after "Light" find Eternal Peace and Activity in the Service of Love. If my present effort in sending these books forth into the world can carry some of the Love, Light, and Happiness I have received to those of earth, who also have been seeking the "Light," I shall have been amply rewarded.

The saying that Truth is stranger than fiction applies to this book. It is for the reader to accept or reject as he chooses but the Ascended Masters, whose help I have received, have said to me often;—"The more humanity can accept our 'Presence,' the wider they open the door for us to pour greater and greater help to them; but the rejection of us, by those who do not agree with this Truth, does not remove us or that Truth from existence and activity in the universe."

Those, who do accept the Truth herein recorded, will find a new and powerful "Force" entering their lives. Each copy carries with it this Mighty "Presence," Its Radiation, and Sustaining Power. All, who study these pages honestly, deeply, sincerely, and persistently, will know and make contact with the Reality of that "Presence" and Power. To those who read this work, I wish to say, that these experiences are as Real and True as mankind's existence on this earth today, and that they all occurred during August, September, and October of 1930 upon Mount Shasta, California, U. S. A.

GODFRÉ RAY KING

THE ASCENSION

By
CHANERA

I feel My God Flame touch my brow,
The Breath of Love—eternal now,
I raise my eyes and lo, I see
My own Great God Self over me.

A dazzling cloud envelopes all,
I hear My Real God "Presence" call,
I feel a surge of Love's great might,
I enter deep its Breath—its Light.

I see within this Pulsing Flame,
I listen, and hear my Secret Name,
I feel the glow—the Great Flame Breath,
I am the Victor over death.

I stand forth free-Ascended now,
To my heart's Light, all things do bow:
I am a Being of Cause alone
And That Cause, Love—The Sacred Tone.

I pour out Life—I lift, I raise,
My heart o'erflows and sings its praise,
My power strengthens and inspires,
My Great Light Rays are God's Own Fires.

I am a Sun, My Love—Its Light
All else grows dim—earth lost to sight;
I know I am just God—The One
The Source—The Great, Great Central Sun.

CHAPTER - I

MEETING THE MASTER

MOUNT SHASTA stood out boldly against the western sky, surrounded at its base by a growth of pine and fir trees that made it look like a jewel of diamond shining whiteness held in a filigree setting of green. Its snow covered peaks glistened and changed color from moment to moment, as the shadows lengthened in the sun's descent toward the horizon.

Rumor said there was a group of men, Divine men in Fact, called the Brotherhood of Mount Shasta, who formed a branch of the Great White Lodge, and that this Focus from very ancient times had continued unbroken down to the present day.

I had been sent on government business to a little town situated at the foot of the mountain, and while thus engaged occupied my leisure time trying to unravel this rumor concerning The Brotherhood. I knew, through travels in the Far East, that most rumors, myths, and legends have, somewhere as their origin, a deep underlying Truth that usually remains unrecognized by all but those who are Real students of life.

I fell in love with Shasta and each morning, almost involuntarily, saluted the Spirit of the Mountain and the Members of the Order. I sensed something very unusual about the entire locality and, in the light of the experiences that followed, I do not wonder that some of them cast their shadows before.

Long hikes on the trail had become my habit, whenever I wanted to think things out alone or make decisions of serious import. Here, on this great giant of nature, I found recreation, inspiration, and peace that soothed my soul and invigorated mind and body.

I had planned such a hike for pleasure as I thought, to spend some time deep in the heart of the mountain, when the following experience entered my life to change if so completely that I could almost believe I was on another planet—but for my return to the usual routine in which I had been engaged for months.

The morning in question, I started out at daybreak deciding to follow where fancy led, and in a vague sort of way, asked God to direct my path. By noon, I had climbed high up on the side of the mountain where the view to the south was beautiful as a dream.

As the day advanced, it grew very warm and I stopped frequently to rest and enjoy to the full the remarkable stretch of country around the McCloud River, Valley, and town. It came time for lunch, and I sought a mountain spring for clear, cold water. Cup in hand, I bent down to fill it as an electrical current passed through my body from head to foot.

I looked around, and directly behind me stood a young man who, at first glance, seemed to be someone on a hike like myself. I looked more closely, and realized immediately that he was no ordinary person. As this thought passed through my mind, he smiled and addressed me saying:

"My Brother, if you will hand me your cup, I will give you a much more refreshing drink than spring water." I obeyed, and instantly the cup was filled with a creamy liquid. Handing it back to me, he said:

"Drink it."

I did so and must have looked my astonishment for, while the taste was delicious, the electrical vivifying effect in my mind and body made me gasp with surprise. I did not see him put anything into the cup, and I wondered what was happening.

"That which you drank," he explained, "comes directly from the Universal Supply, pure and vivifying as Life Itself, in fact it is Life—Omnipresent Life—for it exists everywhere about us. It is subject to our conscious control and direction, willingly obedient, when we Love enough, because all the Universe obeys the behest of Love. Whatsoever I desire manifests itself, when I command in Love. I held out the cup, and that which I desired for you appeared.

"See! I have but to hold out my hand and, if I wish to use gold—gold is here." Instantly, there lay in his palm a disc about the size of a ten dollar gold piece. Again he continued:

"I see within you a certain Inner understanding of the Great Law but you are not outwardly aware of It enough to produce that which you desire direct from the Omnipresent Universal Supply. You have desired to see something of this kind so intensely, so honestly, and so determinedly, it could no longer be withheld from you.

"However, precipitation is one of the least important activities of the Great Truth of Being. If your desire had not been free from selfishness and the fascination of phenomena, such an experience could not have come to you. When leaving home this morning, you thought you were coming on a hike, that is, so far as the outer activity of your mind was concerned. In the deeper—larger sense—you were really following the urge of your Inner God Self that led to the person, place, and condition wherein your most intense desire could be fulfilled.

"The Truth of Life is you cannot desire that which is not possible of manifestation somewhere in the universe. The more intense the feeling within the desire, the more quickly it will be attained. However, if one is foolish enough to desire something that will injure another of God's children or any other part of His Creation, then that person will pay the penalty in discord and failure somewhere in his own Life's experience.

"It is very important to realize fully that God's intent for every one of His children is abundance of every good and perfect thing. He created Perfection and endowed His children with exactly the same power. They can create and maintain Perfection also and express God—dominion over the earth and all that is therein. Mankind was originally created in the Image: and Likeness of God. The only reason all do not manifest This dominion is because they do not use their Divine Authority—that with which each individual is endowed and by which he is intended to govern his world. Thus, they are not obeying the Law of Love by pouring out peace and blessing to all creation.

"This comes about through their failure to accept and acknowledge themselves—Temples of the Most High Living God—and to hold this acknowledgment with eternal recognition. Humanity—in its present seeming limitation of time, space, and activity—is in the same condition a person in need would be to whom some one held out a handful of money. If the needing one did not step forward and accept the money held out to him—how in the world could he ever have the benefit—which it could bring.

"The mass of mankind is in exactly this state of consciousness today—and will continue in it—until they accept the God within their hearts as—the Owner—Giver—and Doer—of all the Good—that has ever come into their lives and world.

"The personal self of every individual must acknowledge completely and unconditionally that the human or outer activity of consciousness—has absolutely—nothing—of its own. Even the energy—by which one recognizes the Great God Within—is radiated into the personal self—by the Great God Self.

"Love and praise—of That Great Self Within—and the attention maintained focused upon Truth—health—freedom—peace—supply—or any other thing that you may desire for a right use—persistently held in your conscious thought and feeling—will bring them into your use and world—as surely as there is a Great Law of Magnetic Attraction in the Universe.

"The Eternal Law of Life is that—'Whatever you think and feel you bring into form; where your thought is there you are—for you are your consciousness; and whatever you meditate upon—you become.'

"When one allows his mind to dwell upon thoughts of hate—condemnation—lust—envy—jealousy—criticism—fear—doubt—or suspicion—and allows these feelings of irritation to generate within him—he will certainly have discord, failure and disaster in his mind, body and world.

As long as he persists in allowing his attention to be held by such thoughts—whether they be about nations—persons—places—conditions—or things—he is absorbing those activities into the substance of his mind, his body, and his affairs—in fact he is compelling—forcing—them into his experience.

"All these discordant activities reach the individual and his world—through his thought and feeling. Feeling often flashes before one is aware of the thought—in the outer consciousness—which he might use to control it, and this kind of experience should teach him—how great is the energy within his many creations—which has accumulated through habit.

"The feeling activity of Life is the most unguarded point—of human consciousness. It is the accumulative energy by which thoughts are propelled into the atomic substance, and thus—do thoughts become things. I tell you—the need of guarding the feeling cannot be emphasized too strongly for control of the emotions plays the most important part of anything in Life, in maintaining—balance in the mind—health in the body-success and accomplishment in the affairs and world of the personal self of every individual. Thoughts can never become things—until they are clothed with feeling.

"The Holy Ghost or Holy Spirit is the feeling side of Life—God—the Activity of Divine Love—or the Mother Expression of Deity. This is why the sin against the Holy Ghost is referred to—as that which brings such great distress—because any discord in the feeling breaks the Law of Love—which is the Law of Balance—Harmony—and Perfection.

"The greatest crime in the Universe against the Law of Love is humanity's almost ceaseless sending forth—of every kind of irritable and destructive feeling.

"One day the race will come to realize and recognize—that the sinister destructive forces manifesting on this earth and in its atmosphere—generated mark you by human thought and feeling—have only entered the affairs of individuals or nations—through the lack of control in the emotions—of everyone's—daily personal experience. Even destructive thoughts—cannot express themselves as action, events, or become physical things—except by passing through the world of feeling; for it is in this phase of manifestation—that the activity of coalescing the physical atom upon thought forms takes place.

"As the noise from a sudden explosion shocks the nervous system of one who hears it—setting up a trembling sensation in the cellular structure of the body—in exactly the same way—do the flares of irritated feeling shock—disturb—and disarrange the finer substance in the atomic structure of the mind, body, and world of the person who sends them out—consciously or unconsciously—intentionally or unintentionally.

"Discordant feeling is the producer of conditions we call disintegration—old age—lack of memory—and every other failure—in the world of human experience. The effect upon the body structure is the same as that produced upon a building—if the mortar holding the bricks together were to receive repeated shocks, and each day those were to be increased. This continued shock would shake apart the particles composing the mortar—the building would collapse into a chaotic mass—and the form be no more.

"That is what mankind is—constantly—doing to the atomic structure of the human body.

"To give expression to the discordant thoughts and feelings in one's self is the course of least resistance, and the habitual activity of the undeveloped—undisciplined—and wilful individual—who refuses to understand the 'Law of his own Being' and bring the personal self—which is but his instrument of expression—into obedience to 'That Law.'

"He—who cannot or will not control his thoughts and feelings—is in a bad way—for every door of his consciousness is wide open to the disintegrating activities— thrown off by other minds and the emotions of other personalities. It takes neither strength, wisdom nor training to give way to unkind, destructive impulses, and the full-grown human beings who do this are but children—in their development of self-control.

"It is a blight upon the Life of mankind that so little control of the emotions is taught humanity from the cradle to the grave. Attention to this particular point is the greatest need—in the Western world today. It is easy to give way to discordant thoughts, feelings, and activities to be sure—because the mass of mankind are submerged as it were—by environment and association entirely created by themselves.

"The individual—through his control of the outer consciousness—must make the effort to rise out of this condition by his own free will—in order to transcend these limitations—permanently—and no one can hope to rid his life and world of misery, discord, and destruction—until he leashes his own thought and feeling. In this way—he refuses to let the Life—flowing through his mind and body—become qualified by the discord—resulting from every little disturbing occurrence in the world about him.

"At first—such discipline does require determined, continuous effort—for the thoughts and feelings—of ninety-five per cent of humanity—run as uncontrolled and free—as a little tramp dog.

"However—no matter how much effort it takes to bring these two activities under control—it is worth any amount of time and energy expended—and no Real—Permanent—Dominion—of one's Life and world can take place without it. It will be my pleasure and privilege to teach you the use of these Higher Laws, and their application will enable you to release True Wisdom and bring about All Perfection.

"The first step to the control of yourself—is the stilling of all outer activity—of both mind and body. Fifteen to thirty minutes—at night before retiring and in the morning before beginning the day's work—using the following exercise—will do wonders for anyone—who will make the necessary effort.

"For the second step:—make certain of being undisturbed, and after becoming very still—picture and feel your body enveloped in a Dazzling White Light. The first five minutes—while holding this picture—recognize—and feel intensely—the connection between the outer self and Your Mighty God Within—focusing your attention upon the heart center—and visualizing it—as a Golden Sun.

"The next step is the acknowledgment:—'I now joyously accept—the Fulness of the Mighty God Presence—the Pure Christ.' Feel—the Great Brilliancy of the 'Light' and intensify It—in every cell of your body for at least ten minutes longer.

"Then close the meditation by the command:—*I am a Child of the 'Light'—I Love the 'Light'—I Serve the 'Light'—I Live in the 'Light'—I am Protected, Illumined, Supplied, Sustained by the 'Light,' and I Bless the 'Light'.*

"Remember always—'One becomes—*that*—upon which he meditates'—and since all things have come forth from the 'Light'—'Light'—is the Supreme Perfection—and Control—of all things.

"Contemplation and adoration of the 'Light' compels Illumination to take place in the mind—health, strength, and order to come into the body—and peace, harmony, and success to manifest in the affairs of every individual—who will really do it, and seeks to maintain it.

"All the way down the centuries—in every age, under every condition—we are told by all who have expressed the greater accomplishments of Life that—the 'Light' is Supreme—the 'Light' is everywhere—and in the 'Light'—exist all things.

"That Truth is just as true today as it was a million years ago. As far back as there is any record of humanity, the Wise and Great Ones of all ages are portrayed with a radiation of 'Light' about them—emanating from the head and body itself.

"This 'Light' is Real—just as Real as the electric lights in your homes. The day is not far distant—when machines will be constructed to reveal the emanation of—'Light' about every individual—to the physical sight of any one—who cares to observe it. Such a machine—will also show the contamination—or discoloration—that becomes a cloud around the—'Light' of God—which the personal self generates—through discordant thought and feeling. This—and this only—is the way by which the energy—of the Great Life Stream—becomes polluted.

"If you will practice this exercise faithfully and—feel it in every atom of your mind and body—with deep, deep intensity—you will receive abundant proof—of the Tremendous Activity, Power, and Perfection—that abides and is forever active—within the 'Light.' When you have experienced this—for even a short time—you will need no further proof. You become your own proof. The 'Light' is—The Kingdom. Enter into It and BE—at peace. Return to the Father's house. After the first ten days of using—this exercise—it is well to do it three times a day—morning, noon, and night.

"We often hear the complaint: 'Oh! I cannot give all that time.' To any who are of that opinion, I wish to say simply this:

"The time the average person spends in criticising, condemning, and blaming—people, conditions, and things—for not being something other than they are—if occupied with this recognition and use of the 'Light'—will make heaven manifest on earth—for the individual who dares to try and has determination enough to maintain it. Nothing is impossible. The 'Light' never fails.

"The 'Light' is God's Way of creating and maintaining Order, Peace, and Perfection throughout His Creation. Every human being on this earth can have all the time he wants in which to do this—when his desire to do it is intense enough. The intensity—in the desire itself—will re-order the world of people, conditions, and things so as to provide that time—if he earnestly wishes to use it for his upward climb. No person in the world is an exception to—That Law—for the intense desire to do anything constructive—when it becomes intense enough—is the God-Power that releases the energy necessary to create and express the thing desired.

"Everyone has the same supreme privilege of contact—with the All-Powerful Presence of God—and it is the Only Power that—ever did—does now—or ever will—raise the personal self and its world—above earthly discord and limitation.

"My Beloved Son, try this with great determination and know—God in You is Your Certain Victory."

As his discourse ended, I began to realize—that he must be one of the Ascended Masters—for he had not only given me proof of his Dominion over the elements by precipitation—but had instructed and explained—as he did it. I sat wondering how it was—that he knew me.

"My Son," he said, answering my thought at once, "I have known you for æons. In raising your thought—by your own conscious effort—it made my coming to you possible at this time. While I have always been in touch with you, when we were both in our finer bodies—your conscious effort of reaching out to some one of the Ascended Masters—opened the way for me to come to you in a much more tangible way—that is—tangible to your physical senses.

"I see you do not quite recognize me—in your outer consciousness. I was present during your birth, at your mother's passing, and was instrumental in bringing you and Lotus together—at the right time—that your attainment might not be delayed. Again—I assisted—in bringing you and your son into association—in this embodiment. However, be patient:

"Sit still a few moments—watch me closely—and I will reveal my identity to you." I did as he requested and—in perhaps a full minute, I saw his face—body—and clothing—become the living—breathing—tangible—"Presence"—of the Master, Saint Germain, smiling at my astonishment and enjoying my surprise.

He stood there before me—a Magnificent Godlike figure—in a white jeweled robe—a Light and Love sparkling in his eyes—that revealed and proved—the Dominion and Majesty that is his.

"This," he explained, "is the body in which I work a great deal of the time—when occupied with the welfare of mankind—unless the work I am doing at the moment—requires closer contact with the outer world of affairs, and in that case—I make my body take on the characteristics and dress—of the nation with which I am working at the moment.

"Oh!" I exclaimed, "now, I know you—for I have seen you many times like—that—at the Inner levels of consciousness."

"My Son," he explained, "do you not see—what Real Mastery—actually is? We—in the Ascended State—can control the atomic structure of our world—as a potter controls his clay. Every electron and atom in the universe—is obedient—to our desire and command because of the God Power by which we control it and of which—we have earned the right—to be the Directors.

"Mankind in the unascended state marvel at these things—but I tell you—it is no more effort—for us to change the appearance and activity of our bodies—than it is for the ordinary human being—to change his clothes. The unfortunate condition in human consciousness—that keeps individuals in their self-created limitations—is their attitude of mind—which either fears or ridicules—what it does not understand—or what is still worse—in its ignorance says—'That is impossible.' A thing may not be probable—under certain human conditions—but the God-Self—which is the Great 'Light'—can change all human conditions—so nothing is—impossible.

"Every individual has the Divine Flame of Life Within him, and—That God-part of him—has Dominion—wherever he moves in the universe. If he—because of his own mental inertia—will not exert the necessary effort—to reorder his age old habits—of mind and body—he goes on bound by the chains of his own forging—but if he chooses to know the God Within himself—and dares—to give that God-Self—all control of his outer activities—he will receive the knowledge once more of his Dominion over all substance—which has been his from the beginning.

"The time has arrived, when many of humanity are rapidly awakening, and they must—in some way be made to understand—that they have lived again—and again—in hundreds—sometimes thousands of lives—each time in a new physical body.

"The Law of re-embodiment—is the activity in human growth—that gives the individual an opportunity to re-establish a balance—in conditions that he has—consciously—caused to be thrown out of balance. It is but—one activity—of the law of compensation—cause and effect—or what might be called—an Automatic Balancing process—governing all forces—everywhere in the universe. The right understanding of—this Law—gives one the explanation of many conditions—in human experience—which otherwise seem wholly unjust. It is the—only—logical—explanation for the infinite complexities and experiences of human creation, and reveals—the operation and the Law—upon which all manifestation rests. It makes one—know that there is no such thing as—chance—or accident. All is under direct, exact, and Perfect Law. Every experience of consciousness—has a former cause, and everything at the same instant is the cause—of a future effect.

"If a man has injured a woman in one life, he is certain to be reincarnated in a feminine form and pass through a similar experience—until he realizes and experiences—that—which he has caused another to endure. The same thing is true—if a woman be unjust or injures a man. This is the only way by which one is compelled—or rather compels himself—to experience both the cause and effect of everything—which he generates in his world. The individual can create and experience whatsoever he will in his own world—but if he chooses to do that which causes others to experience discord, then he—compels himself—to go through a similar condition—until he understands—what the effect of his own creation is—upon the rest of the Life of the universe.

"Come with me, and we will review the physical life in which you used a feminine form in France—wherein you were a singer of splendid accomplishment with a voice of rare beauty and power."

Immediately—without the least effort on my part—I stood outside my physical body—seeing it clearly—as it reposed upon the ground. I wondered, if it would be safe there on the mountainside, and in answer to my thought, Saint Germain replied:

"Do not be disturbed. Not a thing in the world can harm your body—while we are away. Observe!"

Instantly, I saw it surrounded by a White Flame—forming a circle about fifty feet in diameter.

He placed his right arm around me, and I saw—we were rising rapidly from the ground—but I soon became adjusted to his vibratory action. There was no definite feeling of motion through space, but presently—we looked down upon a village in the south of France, and he continued:

"Here, you were born as an only child—the daughter of a beautiful woman, whose life was an example of Idealism far in advance of the majority in that period. Your father was a most devoted husband and companion, highly cultured, and inspired by the early Christian Spirit.

"The atmospheric ether of every environment records all that has ever transpired—in that locality. I will revivify—these Etheric Records—and you shall see—living pictures—giving every detail of your life.

"You sang at the church of this village and studied with a teacher, who persuaded your parents to let her give you training. You made rapid progress, and then received still greater advantages, when they moved to Paris. After a year of intensive study, an opportunity came to sing before the Queen of France, and through her patronage you had appearances at many of her salons. This assured you a successful musical career. France and success lavished their gifts upon you for the next five years, and you accumulated much wealth.

"Suddenly, both parents passed through the change called death, and the shock to you, was very great, followed by many weeks of serious illness. When you recovered and returned again to concert work, a new sympathetic quality had come into your voice, through the recent experience of grief.

"A man, who had guided much of your musical study, became director of your public work, and you came to depend upon him as one who seemed worthy of trust. Then followed fourteen years of brilliant success, at the end of which you became suddenly ill and passed on within a week. Your jewels and wealth were left in care of the director to be used to help others, and to fulfill certain plans for which you had worked all your life. The last rites were no sooner over, than a complete change took place within him. Greed took possession entirely. Now, I shall show you that man whom you met some years ago here in America in your present life. The incident in business, I am quite sure you remember clearly."

Here, he showed me a business association in which I had tried to help several people while in the West some ten years previously, in connection with a representative from the Belgian government.

"That man," he continued, "was given a chance here to right the wrong he did you in France. He was shown the condition, and knew full well the situation for we showed it to him, but he was not yet strong enough to permit the working out of the Great Cosmic Law of Justice and balance that debt. If he had done so of his own volition, it would have given him freedom in many ways and enabled him to have progressed much more rapidly in this embodiment."

Thus, does the outer life keep the individual bound to the wheel of necessity, rebirth, continued struggle, and pain until we—let—the "Light of the Christ Within"—illumine and purify us that we may respond only to the Plan of God—Love, Peace, and Perfection for His Creation. This is the kind of lesson—one never forgets—because objective teaching records the experience in the—vision—as well as in the mind. The record in the sight is deeper and—necessarily receives more attention—from the outer activity of the intellect.

The essence of that long forgotten experience certainly fixed itself in my memory—permanently—for I can recall every detail of it to this day, as clearly as when I observed it with him.

"Now," he went on, "we will recall another of your embodiments—one that you had in Egypt."

We rose from the earth, and moved rapidly forward. I was very conscious of the Mediterranean, as we passed over its beautiful waters. We went on to Karnak and Luxor—then again came into contact with the earth.

"Watch closely," he said. "This record is of a very ancient temple in Luxor—not among those whose ruins the archæologists are exploring today but one antedating any that have been discovered so far. If they knew where to look—they would find magnificent temples in a state of almost perfect preservation."

Indicating a certain spot filled with ruins—which is all that travellers can see today—the scene became replaced by the activity in the ether, as it had originally been—in all its beauty and splendor—far more magnificent than anything of which the present generation has any concept.

The gardens and pools were surrounded by great pillars of white marble and rose granite. The entire locality became Living—Real—Vibrant—and just as tangible as any physical city on earth today. It was so perfectly natural and normal that I asked—how he made these experiences so vivid?

"Man and his creations," he replied, "as well as Nature, have an etheric counterpart—a pattern—which makes its eternal impression upon the atmosphere about him—wherever he goes. The pattern of the individual's activity and life experience is—within his own aura all the time. A similar record exists in the aura of every locality. An Ascended Master may—if he chooses revivify or reclothe the individual's record of former activities—wherever that person happens to be—for the pattern upon which the Master coalesces the atomic structure—is always in the aura of that individual. When the Master reclothes—the record of a locality—he must do it in the same specific place—for such a record, when reclothed—becomes the same living form and structure—that it was—when first built in physical substance.

"In this way—it is possible to coalesce again the physical structure of entire buildings—and their surroundings—when the Ascended Master so desires—for the accomplishment of some good purpose. When one has attained this God-Given Dominion—he can and does—reclothe and reanimate—any Etheric Record he desires to make visible—for the instruction and benefit of students and others.

"When he does this—it is as Real as Reality Itself—and the reclothed objects can be photographed, handled and made physically tangible—to the physical senses of the one observing them.

"Notice!" he reminded me, "you are experiencing these activities in your finer body—but they are none the less—Real—because of that—for your physical body is only a garment which you—the Self-Conscious—thinking—and experiencing individual, wear.

"It is the same as though you wore a heavy overcoat in the cold winter atmosphere and only a light suit of clothes on a very warm summer day.

Experiences in your light suit of clothes—would surely be no less—Real—than those you lived through in your heavy overcoat. I call this to your attention, that you may understand—the fuller—and less limited—activities of Life." We examined the grounds, the surrounding country, and architecture.

"Come, let us enter," he said, and as he spoke, stepped forward and passed through the main entrance into the temple itself. We then became living actors and—at the same time observers—of the following experience. We passed into the main part of the temple, and proceeded toward the Inner Sanctuary. The High Priest came directly up to us, and seemed to know me.

"This priest of ancient days," Saint Germain explained, "is now your son." A lesser priest appeared whom I immediately felt I knew, and he remarked:

"The assisting priest was yourself." We entered the Inner Sanctuary and saw the vestal virgin guarding the—Sacred Fire. She—whom I now beheld was Lotus—my beloved Twin Ray—whom I met and married some years ago and—who is the mother of our son.

The scene changed—and we saw a visiting prince from a distant province—plan to seize the vestal virgin for his bride. All seemed to go well, until the High Priest was shown a vision—of what was about to take place. It disturbed him—but he kept his own counsel.

Standing guard—as the slaves of the prince entered—he watched them approach the Sanctuary. As they came nearer—he stepped forward and spoke but one word, that meant

"Stop!"

One slave—bolder than the rest—came on. The High Priest warned him back—but still he came nearer. When he reached a certain Sacred Circle of force—which emanated from the Altar—the priest no longer hesitated. He stepped to the outer-edge of that Protecting Radiance—raised his right hand—and pointed directly at the slave.

A flash of Flame shot forth like lightning—and the slave fell lifeless to the floor. The prince, who was watching, came forward—in an insane rage.

"Stop!" commanded the priest again—in a voice like a clap of thunder. The prince hesitated for a moment—stunned by the very power of the word—and the priest continued:

"Listen to me! You shall—not—desecrate the highest of God's Gifts—to the Temple of Life. Begone! before you follow the example—of your too brazen and misdirected slave."

The High Priest was fully conscious—of the power he could wield and—as he stood watching the prince—he was the very embodiment of self-control—of Illimitable force—consciously held in obedience to his will. He was Majesty—crowned with Eternal Power.

The will of the prince was powerful also—but he had no control over himself and—as another wave of blind rage swept over him—when he found himself again opposed—and giving full vent to lust—he rushed forward.

The priest—quick as a flash—raised his hand. The Flame flashed out a second time—and the prince followed the fate of his former slave.

Saint Germain turned to me, and explained the experience still farther.

"You see," he began, "that is the way the quality within every force—reacts—upon the one who sends it out. The prince and his slave came with the qualities of hate, selfishness, and depravity within their feelings and—when the priest directed the force—of which he was the master—toward them—it took on their qualities—the moment it touched their auras. He merely turned their own feelings and selfishness—back upon themselves. The priest—in his unselfish effort to protect another—was himself also protected."

That incident closed, the scene of splendor vanished, and again we stood amidst the temple ruins. Saint Germain revealed still more to me, which may not be recorded here.

"There is only one way," he went on, "to avoid the cosmic wheel of cause and effect—the necessity for re-embodiment—and that is through the conscious effort to comprehend—the Law of Life. One must earnestly seek the God Within—make permanent, conscious contact with that 'Inner Self'—and hold firmly to it—in the face of every condition in the outer life. It will be my pleasure and privilege to show you more—but only for the instruction it will bring—to yourself and others. Come! We must now return." As we came near my body, he instructed again:

"Watch the circle of White Flame disappear!" I looked—it vanished—and a moment later I was back in my body. The sun was sinking, and I knew it would be nearly midnight by the time we arrived home.

"Place your arm about my shoulder," said Saint Germain, "and close your eyes." I felt my body lifted from the ground, but I was not particularly conscious of moving forward. Presently, my feet touched the floor and opening my eyes—I stood in the lodge. Saint Germain was greatly amused, when I asked—how it was that we could come back in this manner without attracting the attention of the people about us—and he answered;

"We many times draw about our bodies the cloak of invisibility, when moving among those in physical form," and the next second he was gone.

I had heard of the Great Ascended Masters who could take their bodies with them wherever they go, and manifest—or bring into visibility anything they desire to use—direct from the Universal. However, to actually experience contact with one of them was a very different thing, and I tried to realize in full the marvel of the experience. To Saint Germain, it was evidently a most ordinary occurrence.

I sat in quiet contemplation for a long time in deep, deep gratitude—trying to comprehend—and fully realize his explanation of—"The Law"—concerning desire. He emphasized its importance and activity as a motive power in the universe, to propel forward new ideas—compelling an expansion of consciousness to take place within the Life of every individual. He had explained it by saying:

"Constructive Desire is the expanding activity within Life—for it is only in this way—that greater and greater ideas, activity, and accomplishment are pushed through—into expression in the outer world of substance and form. Within every—Right Desire—is the power of its fulfillment. Man is the Son of God. He is commanded—by the Father—to choose how he shall direct the—Life energy—and what quality he wishes his fulfilled desire to express. This he—must—do for free will is his birthright.

"It is the function—of the outer activity of the intellect—to guide—all—expansion into constructive channels. This is the purpose and duty—of the outer self. To allow the Great Life, or God Energy, to be used only for the gratification of the sense desires—the habit of the mass of mankind—is its destructive use and is always—without any exception—followed by inharmony, weakness, failure, and destruction.

"The constructive use of desire is—the conscious direction—of this limitless God Energy—by Wisdom. All desire directed—by Wisdom—carries some kind of blessing to the rest of creation. All desire—directed by the God Within—goes forth with the feeling of Love and blesses always." The next few days, I spent writing this record of my experiences. Then one morning on awakening I found a golden card lying on the table near my couch. It looked like a piece of metallic gold and on it in beautiful shaded script of a lovely violet color—was just one short sentence:

"Be at our trysting place on the mountain at seven in the morning," signed, "Saint Germain."

I put this card away carefully, and could scarcely wait the intervening time—so great was my expectancy. Early the next morning, while preparing a lunch, there came a distinct impulse—not to take anything with me. I obeyed, and decided—to trust—that my needs would be supplied directly from the Universal.

Light of heart, I was soon on my way, determined not to miss any opportunity to ask questions—if permitted. As I approached the appointed place—my body became lighter and lighter—until by the time I was within a quarter of a mile—my feet scarcely touched the ground. There was no one in sight, so I sat down on a log to wait for Saint Germain—feeling no fatigue whatsoever—although my hike had been about ten miles.

As I contemplated the wonderful privilege and blessing that had come to me, I heard a twig crack and looked around expecting to see him. Imagine my surprise, when not fifty feet away, I saw a panther—slowly approaching.

My hair must have stood on end. I wanted to run—to scream—anything—so frantic was the feeling of fear within me. It would have been useless to move for one spring from the panther would have been fatal to me.

My brain whirled so great was my fear—but one idea came through clearly—and held my attention steady. I realized—that I had the Mighty "Presence of God" right within me and—that this "Presence" was all Love. This beautiful animal was a part of God's Life also, and I made myself—look at it—directly in the eyes. Then came the thought that—one part of God could not harm another part—and I was conscious of this fact only.

A feeling of Love swept over me, and went out—like a Ray of Light—directly to the panther—and with it went my fear. The stealthy tread ceased—and I moved slowly toward it—feeling that God's Love filled us both. The vicious glare in the eyes softened—the animal straightened up—and came slowly to me, rubbing its shoulder against my leg. I reached down and stroked the soft head. It looked up into my eyes for a moment and then, laid down and rolled over like a playful kitten. The fur was a beautiful, dark, reddish brown, the body long, supple and of great strength. I continued to play with it and when I suddenly looked up, Saint Germain stood beside me.

"My Son," he said, "I saw the great strength within you or—I would not have permitted so great a test. You have conquered—fear. My congratulations! Had you not conquered the outer self, I would not have allowed the panther to harm you—but our association would have ceased—for a time.

"I did not have anything to do with the panther being there. It was part of the Inner operation—of the Great Law—as you will see before the association with your new found friend ceases. Now, that you have passed the test of courage, it is possible for me to give—much greater—assistance. Each day you will become stronger, happier, and express much, greater freedom."

He held out his hand, and in a moment there appeared four little cakes of a beautiful golden brown—each about two inches square. He offered these and I ate them at his direction. They were most delicious. Immediately—I felt a quickening, tingling sensation through my entire body—a new sense of health and clearness of mind. Saint Germain seated himself beside me and my instruction began.

CHAPTER - II

The Sahara Desert

"INSTEAD of going forth from the body as in your recent experience, today we will use—the Projected Consciousness," he remarked, as he placed the thumb of his right hand between my eyes and the rest of his fingers over the top of my head. A feeling like a powerful electric current passed over my entire body. Removing his hand, he continued:

"I wish you to fix firmly in mind, and recall frequently for contemplation—the fact—that the Laws I explain, and teach you to use, are to bring you into a condition—of Conscious Mastery—over all forces—and things on earth. This means that—no matter what is being experienced—you are always at every instant in complete, conscious control of your own mind and body, and able to use your own free will—at all times.

"In this state of Projected Consciousness—you are completely conscious and have full mastery overall—your faculties every instant. There is nothing whatsoever—about any of this instruction and its use—that is either of the trance or hypnotic condition at any time, for in both trance and hypnosis the experiencing individual's Conscious Will is not functioning—which is a most dangerous and disastrous activity—to anyone—who permits it to take place in his mind and body.

"There is—no—Conscious Mastery or Dominion—in trance or hypnotic practices, and they are—most—uncertain and dangerous—to the Soul Growth—of the one who permits such practice. Please understand thoroughly—that the Conscious Control, Mastery, and use—of the forces and things on this earth, should at all times be under the direction of your—Inner—or God Self—through the perfect co-operation and obedience of—all—outer faculties in both mind and body, to that—Inner Guidance.

"There is no such thing as Mastery without this, and those known as the—Ascended Masters—never—never—intrude any activity upon the God-Given prerogative of the individual's free will.

"A student may be given the experience of Projection—if an Ascended Master chooses to expand his consciousness temporarily—so that he experiences things happening in two or more places at the same time. In such a condition—the student's faculties are—completely—under the control and direction of his own free will—at every moment. He is fully conscious and active—wherever his body may be—and also at the place—to which the Ascended Master chooses to direct his attention for the instruction.

"The reason—an Ascended Master temporarily raises the consciousness of the student—is to show him how he may do this same thing for himself—by his own effort—consciously, and at will.

"Projected Consciousness is—but increasing the rate of vibration—of the atomic structure in both the mind and body of the student. This is done by the—Radiation—from an Ascended Master—and is an activity of the—'Light'—which increases the vibratory rate—up to the keynote—he sets for the experience. In the higher rate, one uses his faculties of sight and hearing—exactly as he does—in daily life—except—that they are expanded—into the next octave or zone above the human.

"Such use of our senses is the same—as we experience every moment of the waking state—because we can become aware of that which is near and that which is distant—at exactly the same instant. The expansion or contraction of our consciousness is dependent—entirely—upon what the individual—desires. This is—always—subject to the free will and—conscious—direction of the student.

"One can—of his own choice—be conscious of a certain tree in his garden—or—of the entire garden. He uses—the same faculty of sight—to observe both, and uses it in exactly the same way. When he wants to see all of the garden—he makes his sight enlarge its activity—until it takes in all he desires. The larger expansion still includes the smaller—so you see—you must—be conscious of the full control of—all—your faculties in both places—at the same time. The activity that takes place is really—an enlargement of the force-field—in which the sight acts.

"The use of your faculty of sight—in this projection or expansion of consciousness—is accomplished by the raising of the vibratory rate in the optic nerve. The whole process corresponds to the thing that takes place—when one uses a field or marine glass.

"In ordinary experience—human consciousness has been accustomed to use its faculties—only within certain zones or force-fields—and the proof of this is—that one can listen to the sound of a person's voice—who is physically present in the room speaking to him—and he can also hear the bell of a telephone ring somewhere else in the house—at identically the same instant. All the faculties of the outer activity are—elastic. They may be used as—either a microscope or a telescope—depending entirely upon the—desire and will—of the individual.

"If he can be conscious of sound in the room in which his physical body stands, and also be aware of sound two or three rooms distant—by exactly the same process—in a still farther expansion of this faculty—he can hear—at a more distant place. To do this—one must increase the vibratory rate—until it reaches into the more distant zone.

"When you contemplate this—Great Inner God Activity—do you not see how—perfectly and readily—the outer senses—merge into the—Inner—and what has been two becomes—*One.*

"This activity of consciousness can be applied to—all—the other senses—as well as those of sight and hearing. Such a raising process is natural, normal, and harmonious—as simple as the tuning of your radios to any desired wavelength. Radio wavelengths and those of sight and hearing—are—parts of the same activity. Sound contains color and color contains sound. In ordinary daily experience—human beings can hear color and see sound—whenever they become still enough.

"Within certain octaves or zones, vibration registers upon the nerves of the eyes and the result is—what we call sight. Others register upon the nerves of the ears and the result is—what we call hearing. The—average—person's eyes only see objects whose vibratory rate comes within these certain octaves—for they do not see below the infra red, or above the ultra violet ray or zone. Through the—Radiation—of an—Ascended Master—the atomic structure of the brain and eye—vibrates fast enough—to expand into the next octave—above the human.

"This same activity can be expanded several octaves farther—either by the Master's Radiation—or at the command of the—Inner—or—God-Self—of the individual. Many persons do have such experiences involuntarily—but rarely understand—what they mean—or how they come about. In cases, where individuals have had moments of Transcendent Consciousness or been highly inspired—this is what has occurred—although they—seldom—recognize the assistance they have been given.

"Projected Consciousness or Vision has nothing whatsoever to do—with mental pictures—produced by suggestions—that exist only in the minds of other human beings. Such thoughts and pictures are but—flashed—directly into the mind of another person—by the one sending the suggestion. It is the same activity that takes place—when one reflects the image of the sun into a mirror—and then—deflects—it upon the wall.

"Suggestion is as different—from Projected Consciousness—as thinking about a place is different from—being—physically present. Projection is—vivid—Living—Real—as when your physical body is going through an experience, for it is the action of your Inner God-Self—with whom the Ascended Master is—ONE—The Supreme."

Saint Germain and I then became observers—and actors—in a scene of long ago. Again, I was—outwardly—conscious of going through experiences shown me in thought, feeling, and action. The entire operation was as—natural and normal—as breathing, and the only—unusual sensation—about it was the feeling—of greater freedom—and a sense of dominion. We both became very still for a few moments, as he revivified the Etheric Records and my instruction began.

"This is the Sahara Desert," he said, "when it was fertile country having a semi-tropical climate."

There were many streams of water carrying abundant moisture everywhere in the land. In the midst of this empire lay the capital, famous throughout the world for its splendor. The executive buildings were placed in the center upon a slight elevation, and from these, the city itself extended equally in every direction.

"This civilization," he went on, "rose to its apex seventy thousand years ago."

We entered the city, and felt an unusual rhythmic activity that gave one a strange sensation of—lightness—while walking. The people all moved about with great ease and grace. I asked Saint Germain the reason for this, and he replied:

"These people remembered their—Source—and knew themselves as Sons of God—hence, were the possessors and operators of power and wisdom that—to you—may seem miraculous—and super-human. Truthfully speaking—there are no such things as miracles—for all is according to—Law—and that, which seems miraculous to the present concept of humanity, is but—the result of the application of laws—to which mankind's present consciousness is—unaccustomed—and so seems strange and unusual.

"When the Reality of Life is—correctly—understood—all manifestation—that seems miraculous to your present consciousness—is found to be just as—natural and normal an experience—as the forming of words are to one—who has learned the use of the alphabet. It is all but the action of an ever-expanding, ever-progressing manifestation—of Life in form—and that comes about at—all—times through an orderly process of—Law—in love and peace.

"No matter how strange, unusual, and impossible an experience—seems—to humanity's present mental state—it is no proof that there is not a Greater Law and a Wiser Intelligence—acting to produce greater wonders of creation and—surrounding us all the time.

"The knowledge—of the greatest minds of humanity—in the outer world today is to this—Great Inner Wisdom and Power—as the understanding of a small child is to the study—of calculus."

In one building of the central group, we found the attendants attired in most gorgeous fabrics of soft, radiant colors, that harmonized with the interior decoration. One of these acted as guide taking us to the central building, and there he presented us to the king of this great people. The king proved to be—Saint Germain.

Beside him stood a young girl, very beautiful. She had hair like spun gold that hung almost to the floor and eyes of a piercing violet-blue. Her entire bearing was one of loving command. I looked inquiringly at Saint Germain, wondering who she could be, and he answered:

"Lotus."

Beside her stood a young man about twenty years of age and a lad perhaps fourteen. The young man was he, whom we had seen as—the High Priest—in the temple at Luxor, and the lad was the lesser priest. These were the children of the king. Again, we four were working together.

"With this glimpse of former lives," he said, "let us enter into the activity of that blessed people. I say blessed advisedly, and you shall soon see why. The majority of them still retained the full conscious use of all their wisdom and power—as Sons of God—and this—they wielded almost without limit—knowing full well from—Whence—they sprang, and to—What—they were heirs.

"The outer was but the instrument of the Divine Self, as it should be, and was only permitted to do that for which it was created. Naturally—the Great Inner Self—could act unfettered and, of course the perfection and activity of that period, was one of magnificent accomplishment."

At the time of this former civilization, the whole empire was filled with great peace, happiness and prosperity. The King-emperor was a—"Master of the Ancient Wisdom"—and a—"Real Cupbearer of the Light." He—ruled by that "Light"—and his empire was the living example of—Perfection.

"For hundreds of years," Saint Germain continued, "this Perfection was maintained—without army or navy of any kind. The control of the people was vested in the care of fourteen—Ascended Masters of Light—two working on each of the Seven Rays. They thus formed points of focus for the Mighty God Activity to be made visible. Under these fourteen—Luminous Beings—were fourteen lesser—Masters—who formed the heads of seven departments, controlling the activities of science, industry and art. Each of the department heads guided the work under his care by conscious and direct contact with the—God—in himself. Hence, direct from their—Source—did all direction and instruction come for those under them. Thus—Divine Perfection—was constantly flowing through without any interference—from the human.

"This form of government was most remarkable, successful, and satisfactory in every way. There has never been anything on earth since that time—which has even approached such heights. In the ancient records, that have come down to the present day, this former civilization is always referred to as the Golden Age—and so it was in every activity of Life.

"In your beloved America—in the not so far distant future—will come forth a similar recognition of the—Real Inner Self—and this her people will express in high attainment. She is a—Land of Light—and Her—Light—shall blaze forth—brilliant as the sun at noonday—among the nations of the earth.

She was a Land of Great Light—ages ago—and will again come into her spiritual heritage for—nothing—can prevent it. She is strong within her own mind and body—stronger than you think—and that strength she will exert to rise out of and throw off from border to border—all—that weighs heavily upon her at the present time.

"America has a destiny of great import to the other nations of the earth and Those—who have watched over her for centuries—still watch. Through Their protection and love—she shall fulfill that destiny. America! We—the Ascended Host of Light—love and guard you. America! We love you.

"A similar form of perfect government—will—come at a later period, when you have cast off certain activities within—that hang like fungi—and sap your strength as a vampire. Beloved ones in America—be not discouraged—when the seeming dark clouds hang low. Everyone of them—shall—show you its golden lining. Back of the cloud that seems to threaten, is the—'Crystal Pure Light of God and His Messengers, the Ascended Masters of Love and Perfection'—watching over America, the government, and her people. Again I say, 'America—we love you.'

"One by one, great awakened souls are coming forth who will become clearly conscious of their own—Mighty, Inherent God-Power—and such as these—will—be placed in all official positions of the government. They will be more interested in the—welfare of America—than in their own personal ambitions and—private fortunes. Thus—will another—Golden Age—reign upon earth, and be maintained for—an aeon.

"In the period, just preceding this, which you have been experiencing, the mass of the people used great airships for transportation purposes. As the development reached a still higher point, they had little need for them, except in the outlying districts. All the official class, because they were the more spiritually advanced souls of that race, were able to go from place to place—in the finer bodies—and do all they desired—the same as in your recent experience at Luxor. They also were able—to transport—the physical body at will—for the use of their power—to overcome gravity—was as natural as breathing is to you.

"Gold was a common commodity in this age, as in all 'Golden Ages,' because its natural emanation is a purifying, balancing, and vitalizing energy or force. It is placed within the earth—by the 'Lords of Creation'— those 'Great Beings of Light and Love'—who create and direct worlds—systems of worlds—and the evolution of the beings upon them.

"The outer mind or intellectual knowledge of humanity, holds within it little—very little—understanding of the—Real—purpose for which gold exists on this planet. It grows within the earth like a plant, and—through it is constantly pouring a purifying, vitalizing, and balancing current of energy—into the very ground we walk upon—as well as into the growth of Nature—and the atmosphere we breathe.

"Gold is placed upon this planet for a variety of uses—two of its most trivial and unimportant ones—being that of using gold as a—means of exchange—and for ornamentation. The far-greater activity—and purpose of it within and upon the earth is—the release—of its own inherent quality and energy to purify, vitalize and balance the atomic structure of the world.

"The scientific world today has no inkling as yet of this activity. However, it serves the same purpose to our earth—that radiators do to our homes. Gold is one of the—most important—ways by which the energy from our sun is supplied to the interior of the earth, and a balance of activities maintained. As a conveyor of this energy—it acts as a transformer—to pass the sun's force into the physical substance of our world—as well as to the Life evolving upon it. The energy within gold is—really—the radiant, electronic force from the sun—acting in a lower octave. Gold is sometimes called a—precipitated sunray.

"As the energy within gold is of an extremely high vibratory rate, it can only act upon the finer and more subtle expressions of Life—through absorption. In all—'Golden Ages'—this metal comes into plentiful and common use—by the mass of the people—and whenever such a condition occurs—the spiritual—development of that people reaches—a very high state. In these ages the gold is—never—hoarded but instead, is widely distributed into the use of the mass—who absorbing its purifying energy—are themselves—raised—into greater perfection. Such is the right use of gold and when this—Law—is consciously understood and—obeyed—the individual may draw any quantity he desires to himself by the use of that—Law.

"Because of the gold deposits in all mountain ranges—one finds health and vigor in Life upon the mountains—that he cannot find at any other place—on the earth's surface. No one ever heard of detrimental effects coming to those—who constantly handle—pure—gold. While in its—pure—state, it is soft and wears away easily, still—that very quality—is the fulfilling of this purpose of which I have just spoken.

"The more advanced of these people produced much gold—by precipitation—direct from the Universal. The domes of many buildings were covered with sheets of pure gold and the interiors decorated with brilliant jewels in curious yet marvelous designs. These jewels were also precipitated—direct from the One Eternal Substance.

"As in all ages past, there was a portion of the people—who became more interested in the temporary pleasures of the senses—than in the—larger—creative plan—of the Great God Self. This caused them—to lose—consciousness of the God Power throughout the land—until it remained active in little more than—the city itself. The capital was called the—'City of the Sun.'

"Those governing—realized they must withdraw—and let the people learn—through hard experience—that all their happiness and good came from—the adoration to the God Within—and they must come back into the 'Light'—if they were to be happy."

The king-emperor—through the Inner Wisdom—seeing that the people were becoming still more deeply enmeshed in the sense gratification, realized that it was no longer the Divine Plan to further sustain the kingdom. He was instructed—by those of greater spiritual authority than himself—to give a banquet announcing his decision to withdraw, and thus—bid his subjects farewell.

He called the councilors together, and gave directions for the banquet, ordering it held in the most magnificent place of the empire, known as—the Jeweled Room—in the king's palace. This was lighted—by self-luminous globes—that emitted a brilliant, white radiance. They were suspended from the ceiling by chains of crystal. While the light within was intense and brilliant—yet it had an extremely soothing effect upon the body—giving those in its radiance a sense of great ease and calm. The light from the central globe set the jewels ablaze—in the sunburst design—that formed the great medallion in the middle of the ceiling.

The large banquet hall was elaborately decorated and set with twenty-four white onyx tables, each seating twenty-four guests. This was the first occasion upon which all the king's councilors and their staffs were to be his guests at the same time. The announcement of the banquet caused 'much comment among the people who discussed it thoroughly—each with his neighbor—but to all it was a mystery—for none was able to discern its purpose.

The evening of the event came at last. No one suspected the sorrow within the heart of the noble ruler—nor did they dream of the change so soon to come upon them. The hour arrived, the guests assembled, and everyone breathed mystery.

The great bronze doors to the banquet hall swung majestically open, and a burst of transcendent music, as if played by a gigantic symphony—in the invisible—came forth, surprising even those—who knew the tremendous power—of their adored monarch. He was looked upon—almost like a God—by the people, so great was their love and admiration for the wisdom and help he constantly poured out to them.

As the triumphal music ceased—the king entered—accompanied by his children. The girl was a vision of loveliness. She wore a gown of soft golden fabric—unlike any material of our modern world. The over-drape appeared as if covered with diamonds for with every movement of her body points of light flashed forth. The golden hair falling over her shoulders was caught with two emerald clasps. On her forehead was a single band of white metal, set with diamonds. In the center was what appeared to be a large diamond but was—really—a powerful condensation of "Light"—focused and maintained there by her father.

The king was the only one in the whole empire—who was entrusted with the use of such—Transcendent—Power. The royal family had never used these—Jewels of "Light"—in their contact with the outer world—until that night. Such use of this power was only permitted—in their private worship—of the Great God Self—of whose "Supreme" Presence—they were keenly and constantly aware.

The ruler and his two sons wore form-fitting garments of the same soft golden fabric as the daughter. These were as pliable as leather but made of metallic gold with breast plates like a great sun of jewels. They wore sandals of the same material, also set with precious stones, and the wonderful—Jewel of "Light" rested upon the forehead of each.

The king gave a signal, and the assembled guests were seated. In a voice majestic and powerful, he poured out an invocation from the depths of his heart to that—"Infinite Supreme One."

"O Thou Mighty Omnipresent Source, Thou who dost govern the Universe, The Flame in each human heart! we give love, praise and gratitude unto Thee for Thine own Life, Light, and Love in all things. We adore Thee, and look only unto Thee, the 'Presence' in all things visible and invisible, evolved and unevolved, Thou ceaselessly flowing stream of Life, Who dost forever pour Thyself into all creation, the One Self in All.

"My heart calls unto Thee as never before to arouse these, my people, to their danger, for of late indifference to Thee is creeping over them like a poisonous breath, producing a soul-sleep and drawing a veil before them that shuts out 'Thy Shining Presence.'

"If they must have the experience that consumes and burns away the dross and clouds of the outer self, then do Thou sustain and at last bring them forth in Thy Eternal Perfection. I call unto Thee, Thou Creator of the Universe—Thou Supreme Omnipotent God."

The king took his seat and all waited in silent expectation. In a few moments the service for each individual appeared before him. Course after course was served—as if by unseen hands—the food coming in marvelous crystal and jeweled containers—then disappearing as soon as the course was finished—followed immediately by the succeeding one. Finally, the most elaborate banquet—the empire had ever known—came to an end. All was silence again, as if in breathless expectancy—anticipating some most unusual occurrence.

The king arose and stood a few moments—calmly waiting. Soon—a crystal goblet—appeared at the right hand of each guest. These were filled with a—condensation of Pure Electronic Essence—and for all who drank it, no matter how far down the ages his life-stream extended or how varied his experiences—he never could completely forget the—"God-Self Within." This soul protection was granted to those at the banquet, as a reward for their faith and loyalty—to the God in themselves—the king—and the empire. The councilors and those present had served sincerely and continuously for the good of the empire—and for that service—soul protection—through the centuries was given to them.

Each lifted his goblet and drank to the "God in himself"—to his own "Flame of the Most High Living One." The proceedings of the banquet were broadcast to everyone in the empire—through a radio similar to that—which we use today. It was no larger than a dinner plate—yet powerful enough—to receive what was happening—at any point on the earth's surface.

After the salutation to the Divine Self in each—all became very still—the atmosphere itself seeming perfectly motionless. In a few moments a—Wondrous "Presence"—slowly became visible—in front of the king.

That "Presence" was a "Cosmic Master" from out the—"Great Silence." A murmur of awe and surprise passed over the assembled guests at his appearance—as they recognized in amazement—one of whom they had heard for many centuries—yet whose visible—"Presence"—none had ever seen. Raising his right hand, he addressed those present and all dwelling within the empire.

"O Children of Earth, I bring you a warning of serious import, at a time of great crisis. Arouse yourselves from the snare of the senses that is engulfing you! Awake from your lethargy, before it is too late! This, my 'Brother of Light' must withdraw and leave you to the experience that you have chosen, and which is slowly enticing you into its many pitfalls. You have opened yourselves to the uncontrolled ignorance and emotions of the outer self.

"You give little attention and still less adoration to your 'Source'—the Supreme, the Mighty, the Radiant, the Majestic, the Infinite Cause of all that is—the Creator and Sustainer of all worlds. You give no gratitude to the 'Great Glorious Presence'—the 'Lord of Love'—for the very Life by which you exist.

"Oh! why are you not even grateful, for the blessings Nature pours out so lavishly, for the abundance that comes to you through this fair land, and from your own wise and unselfish ruler? You thank each other for favors—the things of the senses and form that are so ephemeral—that pass from one to another and then are no more—but why, Oh why! do you forget the—'Source'—of all Life, all Love, all Intelligence, all Power?

"People! O People! where is your gratitude to Life for Love, for the magnificence of experience that you enjoy every moment, every hour, every day, year after year? All this you call your own, but it has always belonged, does now, and always will belong to the—One Great Source of Life, Light, Love and All Good—GOD—the Supreme—the Adorable—the All-Pervading One.

"When by your own misuse of the energy of Life—which this All-Pervading One showers upon you constantly, pure, perfect, and uncontaminated—you have created conditions so destructive and painful that they can no longer be endured—you turn in either desperation, agony, or rebellion and call upon—God—for relief from your misery. This is your offering to the—'Giver of all Good'—in return for that Ceaseless Perfection which he continually bestows in—Supreme Love. The only condition, upon which the—'One Great Self'—gives all, is its right use—that it may bless the rest of creation with infinite joy, harmony and activity.

"When in the depths of misery—you turn again to your Source, for relief from your misdeeds—you either cry in the agony of despair or, if rebellious, blame—Life—and the—Source of All Good—for allowing, what you call injustice and wrong conditions to exist in you and your world.

"It is you, the little personal self—who are unjust to Life—you who are unfair—you who create the misery of earth, for only humanity—because it has free will to create as it chooses—each individual through his own thought and feeling—only humanity—who dares to bring into existence the discord, misery, and deformity that express upon earth. This is a blight upon Creation and the Perfection that forever swings in the—Great Cosmic Melody of Eternal Song.

"Only mankind is guilty of making a discord in the music of the spheres, for all else lives and acts in accordance with the—'Law of Love, of Life, of Harmony, and of Light.' All else blends into the harmonious whole—the 'Body of the Infinite, All-Loving One.'

"All other realms of—'Life and Light'—move and create according to the fundamental principle upon which all Perfection rests. That principle is Love. If it were not for the—'Great Selfless Ones'—like your ruler—the Great Host of Ascended Masters—whose very keynote of existence is Love—humanity would long ago have destroyed itself and the very planet upon which it exists.

"The transcendent and magnificent activities of Love and Light are the Natural Conditions in which God created and expected His human children to manifest—obeying His command—'to Love.' There is no such thing as a supernatural condition anywhere in the universe. All that is Transcendent, Beautiful and Perfect is Natural and according to the 'Law of Love.' Anything other than that is sub-natural. The daily experience of the Host of Ascended Masters is—the Perfection—God's children were meant to live in always. Earth's children did express this Perfection once—in a former cycle, which was—'One Golden Age.'

"That former civilization—that Ancient Perfection—is older than you dream—older than you believe the planet to be. All mankind at that period lived in a similar transcendent state, as the Ascended Masters, and the condition of misery, that has followed since that time down through the ages, came about because they chose to look away from their 'Source'—Love—as the plan by which to live Life.

"When the children of earth look away from Love—they are deliberately and consciously choosing the experience of chaos. Whoever seeks to exist without—Love—cannot survive long—anywhere in creation. Such efforts are bound to bring failure, misery, and dissolution. By its very condition—it must return to chaos—the unformed—so it may be used over again in combination with Love, and thus produce a new form.

"This is the 'Law of Universal—as well as individual Life.' It is Immutable, Irrevocable, Eternal, yet Beneficent, for creation in form exists that God may have something upon which to pour out—Love—and so express in action. This is the 'Law of the Mighty One' from which all else proceeds. It is the 'Mandate of Eternity' and the Vastness and Brilliance of that Perfection cannot be described in words.

"If there were not these Actual, Real, Permanent and Perfect conditions of Life and experience, which far transcend human description—existence would be but a travesty upon the stupendous activity of Life—that swings forever throughout creation. There are those higher, harmonious, Transcendent Spheres—realms of activity and consciousness—individual and cosmic—where creation goes on continually in Joy, in Love, in Freedom, and in Perfection.

"These are Real, Real, Real and much more permanent than your bodies and buildings in the physical world about you. These Realms of Life are created of Substance which is so charged with—Love—that they can never have a quality or activity of discord, imperfection, or disintegration imposed upon them or registered within them. Because they are based upon Love, the Perfection of such a manifestation is forever maintained, ever active, ever expanding, ever blessing with the joy of all that exists.

"You bring woe upon yourselves—which propels you into embodiment again and again in the ignorance of the senses, the human appetites, and desires of the outer self. These appetites in the feeling nature of mankind are in themselves but an accumulation of energy which the individual through his thought and feeling has given a quality of one kind or another. This misqualified energy, gathers a momentum through human expression and becomes habit. Habit is but energy specifically qualified and held focused for a time upon one objective.

"The sense appetites of former lives become the driving forces and habits of the next—keeping you slaves, bound to the chariot wheels of discord, lack, and necessity—whirling you through a maze of human problems and experiences of your own creation—compelling you to learn and obey the—'Law of the One'—'Love.'

"Your own miscreations drive you on, and on, and on, until you are willing to understand Life and obey Its—One Law—Love. You whirl through Life after Life, experiencing discord upon discord, until you do learn to live the 'Law of Love.'

"This is a compelling activity—which none escape—and it continues until the outer self asks-the reason—for its misery, and understands that its release from the experience of suffering can only come through—obedience—to the 'Law of Love.' Such obedience begins as calm, peace, and kindliness in the feelings—whose center is in the heart. Its contact with the outer world must come through the 'Inner Feeling.'

"Love is not an activity of the mind, but is the—'Pure and Luminous Essence'—which creates mind. This—Essence—from the—Great God Flame—streams into substance, and constantly pours itself out, as Perfection in form and action. Love is Perfection manifest. It can only express peace, joy, and an outpouring of those feelings to all creation—unconditionally. It asks—nothing—for Itself because It is—Eternally Self-Creating—being the Heartbeat—of the 'Supreme.' Love owns—All—and is only concerned with setting the Plan of Perfection into action in all. Thus, It is a constant pouring out of Itself. It takes no cognizance of what has been given in the past, but receives Its joy and maintains Its balance by the continual—Out-streaming of Itself. Because this Perfection is within Love—forever flowing forth—it is incapable of recording anything but Itself.

"'Love' alone is the basis of harmony and the right use of all Life energy. In human experience, this grows into a desire to give, and give, and give of all the individual's peace and harmony unto the rest of creation.

"People! O People! forever throughout the ages! only enough Love can bring you back to the Heaven you once knew and abided in. Here, you will once again embrace the fulness of the 'Great Light' that gives all through Love.

"A visiting prince approaches your borders. He will enter this city—seeking the daughter of your king. You will come under the rule of this prince but the recognition of your mistake will be futile. Nothing can avail, for the royal family will be drawn into the protection and care of those—whose power and authority are of God—and against whom—no human desire can ever prevail. These are the Great Ascended Masters of Light—from the Golden Etheric City—over this land. Here your ruler and his beloved children will abide for a cycle of time." Turning to the king he addressed him, saying:

"I bless you my noble, patient Brother! Loving and selfless has been the service to your people. Deep and eternal is your devotion to the Supreme One—the Source of All Creation. The Golden Etheric City awaits and joyously welcomes you and your children.

"Within Its radiance you shall live serving through the Rays of Light which are forever streaming out from those who dwell therein, until these your people shall redeem themselves by—obedience—to the 'Law of Love.'

"This 'Empire of Light' exists over the land you have loved so well. It is composed of self-luminous, etheric substance and rests above the physical city which is your capital. It is Real, very Real and much more permanent than any earthly city, for—'Light'—is indestructible and the Golden City is made of—'Light.' Into It, no inharmonious thought or disturbing condition of any kind can ever enter.

"I will return in seven days to take you and your children into the—'City of Light'—where we shall watch the progress of humanity, and draw into the—'Light'—all who will discipline and make themselves ready. Encircling the City is—an invincible belt of electronic force—through which it is impossible for anything uninvited to pass."

When he had finished speaking, he blessed the royal family, the guests and the empire and, in the moments of silence that followed—His Light—and the outline of His Body within it—grew fainter and fainter until it disappeared entirely.

A murmur passed through the great banquet hall, and as all looked toward the king, his head was bowed in reverent silence. Then he slowly rose and bid his guests good-night.

On the seventh day, the—"Brother from out the Silence"—returned and enfolding the king and his children within his own blazing aura, withdrew into the—"Golden Etheric City of Light."

The visiting prince arrived the next day, discovered the condition of the empire, and the consternation that still held sway over its people. He at once subtly planned to become its ruler. This he accomplished without opposition. Two thousand years later—most of that empire had become barren land, the streams dried up, and desolation stretched everywhere—all the result of the discord and selfishness of mankind and the blight it becomes upon the growth of plant life in nature. This kingdom had extended the entire width of Africa on east—until it reached the Himalayan Mountains.

There followed a great cataclysm—submerging all the land. Through that change, an inland sea was formed where the Sahara Desert now lies. Another earth change, which took place about twelve thousand years ago—drained this sea—and a part of it later became the present Sahara Desert. The River Nile, as it is today, most nearly resembles the beautiful streams—of that long forgotten period.

Thus ended our observation of those very ancient scenes. I could hardly believe my senses—I was so astonished at the way the experiences of the past were revivified—the pictures projected in all three dimensions—and the activity of the people in that remote age portrayed.

Realizing how surprised and unaccustomed to such activities I was—Saint Germain promised to take me to the physical records of that period and its people—and give me physical proof—that it was not—a vision—conjured up by him.

Glancing around from the log upon which we were seated, we saw the panther lying nearby fast asleep. Saint Germain took up the explanation of several important phases on the application of higher laws, for the manifesting of one's own inherent dominion over the things of the sense world. This led to how he was able to express such youth and Perfection in a body so old—according to the way human beings count time.

"Eternal Youth," he explained, "is the—Flame of God—abiding in the body of man—the Father's gift of Himself—to His Creation. Youth and beauty of both mind and body can only be kept—permanently—by those individuals—who are strong enough to shut out discord, and whoever does—that—can and will express—Perfection—and maintain it.

"Where Peace, Love, and Light do not abide within the thoughts and feelings of a human being—no amount of physical effort can possibly keep the outer self—expressing youth and beauty. These exist—Eternally—within the God Flame which is the—Divine Self—of every individual. Whatever discord the outer self allows to flash through the thought and feeling is—that—instant stamped upon the flesh of the physical body. Eternal Youth and Beauty are Self-Created and—forever Self-Existent—within the Flame of God's Life—in every human being. This is—God's Plan—for manifesting—His Perfection—into the world of form and maintaining it forever.

"Youth, Beauty, and Perfection are attributes of Love which the—God Principle—is continually pouring forth into—Its Creation. Within each individual is placed the power and means for—maintaining and increasing—that perfect ever-expanding activity of creation.

"The power of accomplishment is the energy of the—God Self—in each human being born into the world. It is always active every moment in your mind, body, and world. There is no instant in which this mighty energy is not flowing through all individuals. You are privileged to qualify it—as you please—at the command of your own free will through consciously directed thought and feeling.

"Thought is the only thing in the universe that can create vibration—and through vibration—you qualify this ever-flowing energy with whatever you desire to have manifest in your life and world. This limitless, intelligent, radiant energy is flowing—ceaselessly through your nervous system—and is the Eternal Life and vitality in the blood stream coursing through your veins. It is an all-powerful, omnipresent, intelligent activity given you by—the Father—the God Principle of Life—to be consciously directed according to your freewill. Real Intelligence—which uses everything constructively—comes only from Within the God Principle—the Flame of Life—and is not merely the activity of the intellect. Real Intelligence is Wisdom or—God knowledge—and this does not and—cannot—think wrong thoughts. Wrong thoughts come only from impressions made upon the intellect by the world—outside—of the individual. If individuals would discriminate between their—own thoughts—that is thoughts from within their own God Flame—and the suggestions, thrown off by other people's intellects and the evidence of the senses which consider appearances only—they would be able—to avoid all discordant activities and conditions—in the world of experience.

"The Light—from within one's own—God Flame is the criterion—the standard of Perfection—by which all thoughts and feelings—that reach us through the five senses—should be tested. No one can keep his thoughts and feelings qualified with Perfection—unless he goes to the—'Source of Perfection'—for that quality and Perfection only abides within the—God Flame.

"This is the individual's need—for meditation upon and communion with—the Light of God—within himself. Pure Life Essence will not only give and sustain Eternal youth and beauty in the body—but will enable you to maintain—Perfect Balance between your God-Self and the outer or personal self. In fact—this Pure Life Energy is the power—which the outer self uses—to hold its connection with its Divine Source—the God Self. In reality—these two are One—except, when the intellect or outer activity of the mind—the sense consciousness—accepts imperfection, inharmony, incompleteness or thinks itself a creation apart—from the All-Pervading One 'Presence' of Life. If the sense consciousness thinks itself something separate from God—Perfection—then that condition is established unto it—for what the sense consciousness thinks into its world—the world returns to it.

"When one lets an idea of imperfection or separation from God occupy his attention, and therefore his mind—a condition corresponding to that begins to express itself in his body and world. This causes the person—to feel—himself an entity apart from his Source. The moment he thinks himself separated from God—he thinks his Life, Intelligence, and Power has beginning and end.

"Life always has been, is now, and always will be. No one can really destroy Life. Through various activities in the mental and physical world—form can be disintegrated or temporarily demolished—but the consciousness of the individual is Eternal; and can control all substance everywhere in manifestation—when the God Life within is acknowledged as the—'Knower, Giver, and Doer' of all good in creation.

"I tell you—Truth—when I say there is only one Source of all Good—God. The conscious recognition and acceptance of this Fact—acknowledged by the—outer activity—of the mind, knot two or three times a day—but every few moments all day long—no matter what the outer self is doing, and this maintained—will enable anyone to express his perfect freedom and dominion over all things human.

"To most people the above sounds difficult—for they have lived so many centuries in the belief that they are beings apart from God—while every instant of every day, they are using—God Life—God Energy—God Substance—and God Activity in everything they think and do without realizing it. However, it requires the conscious admitting of this fact in the outer activity of the mind, and constructive direction, to release Its Full Power—through the personal self.

"Recognition, conscious direction, and constructive use of the—God Energy—maintained within one's self at all times—is the way of Perfection, Mastery, and Dominion over all things on earth—including the conscious control of—all—natural forces. The instruction I have been giving you will erase completely all false beliefs—if maintained. The rapidity with which it is accomplished depends upon how continuously, persistently, and deeply you feel and associate with your—God Self.

"In the attainment of Mastery or Adeptship—the conscious control of all force and manipulation of substance are dependent first—upon the acknowledgment of your own individual God Self; second, upon perfect calmness of feeling—under all circumstances; and third, one must be passed—all—temptation of misusing power. The stilling of all emotions at the command of the conscious will is imperative—and the demand for it in the Adept is unconditional—if Dominion is to be attained.

"It does—not—mean a repression of discord within one's self at any time—but is a stilling and harmonizing of the feelings—no matter what the circumstances are—which surround the mind or body of the student. Such control is not an easy thing for humanity in the Western World—because the temperament—of most people in the Occident is sensitive, emotional, and impulsive. This characteristic is energy of tremendous power. It must be controlled—held in reserve—and released only through conscious direction—for the accomplishment of something constructive. Until the waste of energy is checked and completely governed—the individual cannot, and never will, make—permanent progress.

"The student often asks, if one reaches a point—while still on the path of attainment—where he rises above the use of affirmation? When an individual sincerely uses affirmation—he brings about a full acceptance of the—Truth—of whatever he affirms—for its use is but to focus the attention of the outer mind—so steadily upon the Truth—that he accepts it fully in his feelings—because feeling is the actual- God Energy released—which manifests the—Truth affirmed.

"The continued use of affirmation brings one to the point where he has such a deep realization of the—Truth in anything—he affirms that he is no longer conscious of it—as an affirmation. One uses an affirmation, mantram, or prayer because he desires something made manifest. Right desire is the deepest form of prayer. Thus—by the use of affirmation—the student raises his outer self into the full acceptance of its Truth and—generates—the feeling by which it becomes—a thing manifest. In this deep acceptance comes the manifestation—for through concentration—the spoken word begins to cause instantaneous activity."

My gratitude to Saint Germain for all I had received was too deep for words. He read my thoughts and feelings as one reads a book, and so we both sat silent for some few moments—in perfect attunement. He roused me from my reverie to watch the gorgeous colors in the western sky—the sunset's afterglow.

I wanted to remain on the mountain all night and return home in the morning, enjoying the sunrise. I had no sooner felt the desire—than a beautiful sleeping bag lay at my feet. It was unlike anything—I have ever seen. I reached down to examine the unusual fabric of which it was made, and to my astonishment—found it glowing and warm. I looked up, and Saint Germain smilingly extended to me—a crystal cup—filled with golden liquid—about the consistency of honey. Obedient to his slightest wish I drank it, and instantly, a radiant glow passed through my body. When I had finished, the cup disappeared in my hand.

"O why could I not keep this lovely creation?" I asked in surprise. "Patience—my Son," he answered, "are not your desires being fulfilled one by one? Your sleeping bag will remain until daybreak, and your friend, the panther, will guard you during the night."

Bowing slightly, and with a smile that was graciousness itself, his body became gradually indistinct and then disappeared entirely. I lay down in the lovely bag and was soon fast asleep. As the rosy tints of dawn touched the eastern horizon, I awoke, and the first thought in my mind was concerning the bag, which I had so much enjoyed. With that thought—it vanished back into the universal substance—from which it had come.

The panther came toward me, and together we turned our footsteps homeward. After walking for some distance, the sound of men's voices caught our ears. The animal sniffed the air, suddenly stopped directly in front of me, and looked up. I reached down and patting him, said:

"Now you may go." He bounded away into the thickly wooded section of the mountain to the right of the trail. I continued on my way without further incident, and at last reached my lodgings shortly after noon, in a state of mind—hard to find words to describe.

I wanted to think—contemplate—digest—and become adjusted to an entirely new set of ideas. The unusual—yet very real experiences—through which I had passed within the forty-eight hours just preceding, were causing me to reorder my entire world. I was happy in the extreme and yet, it seemed as if another universe had manifested itself around me. There was the same old prosaic world on the outside that I had always known—to be sure, and yet—was it? Within it all the time had been these wonderful experiences—this tremendous power—these marvelous revelations of freedom and dominion over—all manifestation—of which I had been so totally unaware.

I had been surrounded all my life by these seeming miracles—to which in my previous years I was as oblivious—as if no such thing existed in creation. I thought and thought, deeper and deeper than I had ever contemplated anything before—in my whole existence.

The dinner hour arrived but I was not hungry. However, to begin the evening meal, I ordered a glass of milk. It was served and a few moments later, as I tasted it—imagine my astonishment—to find that it had become—the same creamy liquid—Saint Germain had first given me.

I finished the meal—returned home, and was preparing my bath before retiring, when suddenly the familiar—electrical signal—thrilled me from head to foot. Involuntarily—I held out my hand—and in a few seconds a small cake of crystal-like substance formed in the palm. I somehow knew this was to be put in my bath, and had no more than dropped the substance into the water—than it immediately bubbled and sparkled—as though alive.

I stepped in, and a tingling sensation—thrilled every cell—in my body. I felt—charged—with a high powered electrical current—that illumined and strengthened—my whole being. My bath finished, I lay down, and soon dropped into a dreamless sleep.

CHAPTER - III

The Royal Teton

FOUR days passed without any unusual occurrence, and I tried to realize fully the deeper significance of my recent experiences. It was just growing dark on the evening of the fifth day, when there was a sound of tapping on the window of my room. I looked out, and on the window sill stood a snow white dove—with a tiny card in its mouth.

I stepped to the window and opened it. The dove walked in and—stood calmly waiting. I took the card and read the message—which was written in the same beautiful script—as the previous one—but this time in gold ink—on a white card. On it were the words:

"Be at our meeting place at seven in the morning," signed, "Saint Germain."

As soon as I had taken the card—the dove flew to my shoulder and rubbed its head against my face—as if conveying a message of love—flew again to the window, and was gone like an arrow. I put the card away carefully, hoping it would remain, but the next morning as I looked for it before starting on my hike—it had been dissolved. The golden card, on which the first message was written, had lasted into the third day for I looked at it several times, hoping I could keep it permanently. When I found it had been returned to the universal my heart sank, so great was my disappointment.

To make the hike of ten miles and be there at seven in the morning, I knew would make it necessary for me to leave shortly after midnight. I arose early, and was on my way at three o'clock. By walking rapidly, I reached the forest just at daybreak. I had not gone far—until a plaintive cry came to my ears. Before realizing it, I answered in the same tone—so involuntary was my response. There was a rush of something through the timber and my friend—the panther—bounded toward me, the very embodiment of joy. I patted it and together we proceeded on our way to the meeting place.

Promptly at seven o'clock, Saint Germain stepped—right out of the atmosphere—greeting me with open arms. Again, he handed me the crystal cup—filled this time with a clear—sparkling liquid. I drank it—and the taste was not like anything I had ever physically experienced before. It was almost like the juice of grape-fruit iced—but sparkling and effervescing. The moment I drank it—a sensation like lightning went through my body—carrying the feeling of its sparkling activity—into every vein.

Saint Germain—then gave the panther a little brown cake—which it quickly devoured. In a moment its hair stood straight up—and he remarked:

"Your friend will never again kill deer."

"For the coming experience and instruction—it will be necessary to leave your body here on the mountain side—because you have not yet called forth the—Inner Power—enough to enable you to take it where we are going today. The panther will be the guard for you and as an extra precaution—I will place the cloak—of invisibility—around both. We will go to the Royal Teton.

"Come."

Instantly—I stood out in my finer body—clothed in a rich garment—of self-luminous, golden fabric.

"Observe carefully—the material in which you are clothed," he continued. "The substance composing the garment you wear has certain, extraordinary qualities and powers of its own—one of which is to enable its wearer—to lift and transport physical objects. The garment itself—possesses pure electronic energy, and can be used to move objects—the same as the force one uses through his physical body. This is a phenomenal activity that—the Great Masters of Light—have given permission to be used—for the first time, on this planet."

For the benefit of my readers, I want to state clearly and unmistakably, that—while I was clothed in a body which did function in four dimensions during these experiences—yet it gave me the ability to feel and handle solid objects in the physical world—the same as every one can do in his own physical body. The body I used this time was—not—that which is sometimes called—the astral body.

We soon reached the top of a majestic mountain that stands sentinel over one of the most beautiful scenic belts in the United States. Vast forests lay beneath us, and great ranges of mountains, with their treasures of mineral wealth still untouched, stretched as far as the eye could see.

Going to a point where huge masses of stone lay in confusion, as if giants had hurled them in a war upon each other, Saint Germain touched a great boulder. Instantly, the enormous mass tipped out perhaps four feet away from its original position. He motioned me to follow. We entered and, to my astonishment, stood before a large bronze door.

"This has been here since before the sinking of Atlantis—more than twelve thousand years ago," he explained.

He stepped forward and pressed certain points on the door. The great mass of bronze weighing many tons swung slowly open, and admitted us into a spacious chamber from which a stairway, cut in the solid rock, led downward. We descended some two hundred feet, and entered another space—circular in shape. Saint Germain stepped across the room to a door opposite the stairs, and placed his right hand against it. As it opened, we stood before the entrance of a tube elevator. The interior looked like frosted silver—and in answer to my thought, he said:

"Yes, but harder and stronger than steel and—indestructible." A flat disc of the same metal, fitting the tube quite closely, rose within it to the level of the floor. The platform was controlled and operated—entirely—by the Master. He stepped upon it, and I followed. The door closed, and we began to descend. It was a long way down, although we did not move rapidly. The platform came to a stop at another bronze door of entirely different design.

"We have descended two thousand feet into the very heart of the mountain," he commented, as we stepped out of the tube.

The space in which we stood was of peculiar design and arrangement. It formed an oblong from east to west—whose northeast and northwest corners had been cut on an angle. This formed an outer court or reception room. The heavy bronze door from the tube elevator opened into the court on the northeast wall.

In the north side were two other large bronze doors exactly alike, entering into a great audience hall. On the northwest wall was still another, a fourth door, like the one through which we had come in. Opposite on the long unbroken stretch of the south wall, hung an immense tapestry.

It was made of most unusual material and, while the weave was coarse, yet the thread or fiber was as soft—as camel's hair. The background was of a delicate cream color and against this were two life-sized figures—representing—God Beings—of Great Majesty and Power. The one on the right was masculine, the other feminine. Both were standing—as if in the act of commanding—Cosmic Forces—to obey their decrees.

The masculine figure wore a full-flowing robe of some rich material, of a deep sapphire blue, banded and heavily embroidered in gold. It was evidently—a robe of state—or symbol of authority. Under the outer robe, was a tunic of golden fabric, metal-like in appearance.

A sunburst of rubies, diamonds, sapphires, and emeralds covered the chest. The waist was encircled by a jeweled belt, and from it hung a panel about twelve inches long. It too was heavily encrusted with the same kind of jewels. The tunic reached to the knees, and the lower edge was trimmed with a band about four inches wide of heavy embroidery, in silk of the same color as the jewels.

The entire effect gave one the impression that the garments were—all—self-luminous. The feet were clad in sandal-like boots of golden leather reaching almost to the knees, very ornate and laced with sapphire blue cords. A band of gold about an inch and a half wide rested half way down upon the forehead, binding the figure's wavy golden hair which hung to about six inches below the shoulders.

The complexion was very fair with a soft pink tint, and the eyes were a deep violet blue. The fingers of the left hand rested lightly over the heart, and the upraised right hand held—a blazing crystal rod of power and authority. The lower end was shaped to a point, and on the top rested a sphere, about three inches in diameter—that gave off rays of sparkling white light.

One knew—unmistakably—that the figure portrayed was in the act of wielding—gigantic power—and was a manipulator—of some Mighty Cosmic Force. The entire appearance suggested fullest youth and yet—the wisdom of the ages spoke through the eyes—of a hoary past.

The feminine figure's robe of authority was a deep violet, banded with golden embroidery similar to that of her companion. The underdress was a soft, golden, shimmering material that came almost to the floor. The thread used in weaving the tapestry to represent the garments must have been the same which had actually composed the material in the original clothing. This—Being—wore a jeweled girdle with its panel reaching about two inches below the knees, and encrusted with the same kind of jewels as those of the masculine figure.

The toe of her right sandal was just visible beneath the edge of the dress and was made of golden leather. Her head-dress was a plain band of gold exactly like his and the eyes were the same violet blue but lighter in shade, her golden hair falling to the knees.

On the chest suspended from a golden chain—hung a large seven-pointed star—cut from a single diamond. In her left hand she held a crystal sphere about six inches in diameter, and in her right uplifted like that of the other figure, was a scepter—of a most strange design. About two thirds of the lower portion was made of gold terminating in a spear-shaped point, the upper third composed—of a crystal-like substance—radiantly luminous. This formed into a design at the top—similar to a fleur de lis—except that the middle point was much longer, and tapered to a slender apex formed by its four facets.

The curved leaf on the right of the central portion was—a beautiful pink—and that on the left—a deep sapphire blue—but the middle one was—crystal white. All were—transparent and glowed—with Light. The gold and crystal like portions blended with each other perfectly—for there was no line of demarcation between the two substances. Her scepter symbolized—the three activities—of the Creative Force.

The crystal ball in her left hand—revealed—the unmanifested Perfection of the future—in Cosmic Activity. Both scepters represented—the drawing and directing—of the Creative Power—into universal substance—for special manifestation. They were radiant and beautiful even in the tapestry, and I could but wonder what they must have been—in Reality. Saint Germain stood patiently waiting while I studied the whole concept—so fascinated was I by the—magnificence—of the entire work.

"These two Great Beings—were the founders of this retreat," he remarked, as we turned and passed through the bronze door on our right, and entered a large room which one realized instantly was used as a great council hall for some kind of sacred, ceremonial purpose.

The whole atmosphere was one of magnificence and beauty. Words utterly fail to convey—that which my eyes beheld—and my feelings experienced. It took me some moments to become accustomed to the—dazzling sight—and the—splendor—of my surroundings.

This room was at least two hundred feet long and a hundred feet wide—with a ceiling about fifty feet high. A soft white light, which Saint Germain explained was—an omnipresent force—that the Great Ones always use for light, heat and power—flooded the entire place. About twenty feet of the side-walls and far end of the room were formed in—white onyx. Where this formation ended, the builders had cut through a great vein—of virgin gold—more than two feet in width.

The main stretch of both side-walls was of a light, blue granite but near the end from which we entered, the natural structure changed into rose granite of a still finer quality. The surface of the walls, ceiling and floor had been—highly polished—evidently by some remarkable process.

The arched ceiling rising some ten feet higher than the side-walls, was inlaid with a most unique design. Directly in the center was—a disc of gold—at least twelve feet in diameter. Filling it so that the points touched the circumference—blazed a seven pointed star—composed entirely of yellow diamonds—a solid mass of brilliant, golden Light.

Radiating from this—Central Sun—were two rings of color—each about twelve inches wide—forming a definite band of Light around the star, and of these the inner band was—rose pink—and the outer—an intense violet. The background, against which this star lay, looked like—golden frost—the star itself sending down long rays of gleaming, crystal Light.

Around this design were placed—seven smaller discs—each about two feet in diameter—representing the planets of our system—and the seven rays of color—within the spectrum of white Light. The surface of every disc was—velvet-like in its softness and only the clearest, most intense, positive shade of each color had been used.

As I learned later, at certain times for special purposes—Great Cosmic Beings—pour through these discs—their powerful currents—of force. Here—it is received—by the Great Illumined and unselfish Ones—known as—the Ascended Masters of Light—who again send it forth to the humanity of our earth. This radiation affects—the seven ganglionic centers within every human body on our planet—as well as all animal and plant life. The background of the entire ceiling was the color of a very clear sky on a brilliant moonlight night—yet the surface was highly refractive.

In the center at the far end of the hall about thirty-five feet from the floor in the wall itself—was a large eye—at least—two feet across. This represented the—"All-Seeing-Eye of the Creator"—forever watching over—His Creation—and from Whom—nothing can be hidden.

A tremendous power was focused through—this eye—at certain times—for the accomplishment—of specific results. I could but wonder—as I contemplated it—what my sensations would be were I to see—That Power—in full operation.

Perhaps forty feet from the far end on the east wall, stretching about seventy feet in length and thirty feet in height—was a panel—of some precipitated material. It had been placed a little more than—five feet above the floor level—and sunken into the side-wall for a depth of two inches—making a concave surface around the entire edge.

The substance composing it—looked like beautiful velvet—of a deep indigo blue—yet it was not a fabric of any kind. The nearest physical material to which one could compare it would be that—of a mineral. This substance—is not—in use in the outer world of mankind anywhere—but it can be and is, sometimes precipitated—by the Great Ascended Masters of Light—for a special purpose.

Saint Germain explained that—the panel had been precipitated—and served as a—universal mirror—for the instruction of Initiates and Inner members of a group of Highly Evolved Beings. These Great Ones work—ceaselessly—helping the humanity of our earth—to become Perfected men and women—and enable them to manifest—in their outer lives—the same great—Perfection and Dominion—as did Jesus Christ.

There is—no—outer—organization—of these—Perfected Beings. Only by—living—and expressing—this Perfection—through self-correction of human weaknesses—and full adoration to the Divine Being Within—can an individual draw himself—into association—with those working at this—high—level of attainment.

"Upon this panel," said Saint Germain, "are projected scenes of earth, pictures in the ethers—the akashic records—and activities taking place on Venus or at any other point—which those instructing—wish to make visible to the students. Such scenes are not only pictures of the past and present—but can portray activities—into the far future. These you shall see later."

We passed through the last door on our right, and entered a room whose dimensions were about eighty feet long, forty wide and twenty high, with an arched ceiling—similar to that in the large hall—from which we had just come.

"The entire interior surface of this room is made of—frosted gold—and the purple and green veining—you see on the walls—as if embossed—is precipitated," he continued.

At the far end and on the side wall to our right, reaching from floor to ceiling, was a framework made—of white metal—that looked like—frosted silver. In this framework resting upon roller bearings, were containers made of the same metal. The lids—of these containers—gave classifications—in hieroglyphics—of the contents on the four spindles within each—the hieroglyphics being embossed upon every lid.

The spindles were at least ten inches long—and around every one—had been wound a ribbon—about eight inches wide—made of pressed gold—alloyed with some material—that made it tough and pliable and yet—no thicker—than a piece of ordinary writing paper. The length—of the ribbons of gold—on the spindles varied—from seven to fifty feet—and on each were characters—as if etched into the gold—by something like a stylus. These characters—had been so perfectly done—as to make the whole appear—like script.

"These records are the fulfilling of my promise to you," said Saint Germain, as he indicated a particular section at the far end of the side-wall. "They describe the city, country, and civilization which once existed where the Sahara Desert is now—during the time in which you were my son—and I the ruler—of that ancient empire. This room contains records of many countries—and the rise and fall—of many civilizations." Handing me one of the spindles he released the fastening, and I found—to my astonishment—that I could read its contents.

"I am enabling you to do this," he continued, "by temporarily—raising your consciousness—and calling forth the hidden memory—the former record—of these experiences which you once lived through. The matter of—knowing God and His Universe—is but a contacting—of the Life-record in every form. All forms contain Life, and within the Light emanation of every form—is recorded—its entire past—which any one may train himself to discover and understand—if he be willing to give—his attention and time to the self-discipline necessary—to still the confusion—in the outer activity—of his every-day existence. This eternal record within all things has existed—from the beginning.

"In ages past, humanity manifested Perfection in every way. This former condition of the race has been chronicled by historians as the—Garden of Eden—Eden or E-Don—meaning Divine Wisdom. As the conscious attention—of the outer activity of the mind—was allowed to rest upon the world of the physical senses—the 'Divine Wisdom'—the All-Knowing—activity of consciousness—became clouded or covered over and the 'Cosmic Divine Plan'—of the individual's life—became submerged. Perfection and conscious control—by mankind over all form—was hidden and forgotten—along with it.

"Man became sense-conscious—instead of God-conscious—and so manifested—that—to which his attention was directed and—which he thought most upon. He—deliberately and consciously—turned his back upon the Perfection and Dominion—with which the Father—endowed him in the beginning. He created his own experiences of lack, limitation, and discord of every kind. He identified himself—with the part—instead of the whole—and of course—imperfection—was the result.

"All mankind's limitation—is the result—of the individual's own misuse of the—God-attribute—of freewill. He—compels—himself to live within his own creations until—by the direct volition of the outer activity of his mind—he again consciously looks back—to his Royal beginning—God—the Great Source of All. When this occurs—man will begin to remember—That—which he once was, and may become again—whensoever he chooses to look once more at the—'Great, Cosmic, Blue-Print'—of Himself.

"The record, you have been enabled to read, described the Life and people—as we saw it taking place seventy thousand years ago. You had much to do with the work of making these records—in several lives—which have not yet been revealed."

We crossed the council hall entering the opposite door, and found a room similar in size to the one we had just left—with two smaller rooms adjoining it on the north wall. In the larger room, covering almost the entire wall surface, was more metal framework filled with containers quite like those in the other room.

"These rooms," he continued, "contain only gold and jewels—that are to be used for a special purpose—which will bless the entire world—when mankind has transcended its—unbridled—selfishness." Here, he drew forth a container—filled with gold coin—and went on explaining. "This is Spanish Gold—lost at sea and we—seeing it would not be recovered by other means—brought it here through the activity of certain forces—which we govern. Later—in a time that is rapidly approaching—it will again be sent forth for use in the outer world.

"In these containers," indicating another section, "gold is stored from the lost continents—of Mu and Atlantis—the ancient civilizations of the Gobi and Sahara Deserts—Egypt—Chaldea—Babylonia—Greece—Rome—and others. If all this gold were to be released into the outer activity of the world—it would compel sudden re-adjustment—in every phase of human experience. At present—it would—not—be the part of wisdom. The Infinite Wisdom and Power of those—Great Cosmic Masters—who have been the guardians of the race since its first appearance upon earth—is almost beyond the comprehension of the human mind.

"No one—in this world—ever accumulated a great amount of wealth—without the assistance and radiation of some—Ascended Master. There are occasions—in which individuals can be used as a focus of great wealth—for a specific purpose—and at such times—greatly added power is radiated to them—for through it—they can receive personal assistance. Such an experience is a—test—and opportunity—for their growth. All unusual accomplishment—that takes place in human activity—no matter what the particular channel may be—is always attained—through the assistance of super-human Love, Wisdom, and Power—from an Ascended Master—because he has transcended all limitations of the physical world and—for this reason—more than ordinary success is due to His greater power—through radiation.

"In 1887—the Ascended Host of Masters established a school—on the Inner planes—for the specific purpose of instructing those who have misused wealth—and revealing fully—the results—of their mistakes. Such—as these—are taken and told the—Truth—concerning the—Universal Law—governing all wealth, and the results that come from influencing others to perpetuate their wrong ideas and mistakes. They are given—complete freedom—to accept or reject—the proof—offered. They—always—accept and abide by the instruction given."

We next entered the two smaller rooms which were also equipped with the same kind of containers only—not as large. These were filled with jewels of all kinds—diamonds, rubies, pearls, emeralds and sapphires classified as to variety and quantity. Smilingly, he turned to me and said:

"Now—you know and understand—that the Great God Self—is—the only—Real Owner and Controller of—all—wealth. That 'Presence' appoints—keepers of His treasures—on every plane of life—whether it be Light, Wisdom, Substance or physical riches. You are calm and poised I see, while we are observing this phase of our activity—and that is well. It reveals your Inner strength and ability to do—what is now ready to be accomplished—as soon as you are prepared outwardly.

"You have been shown—proof—that it is we—who really govern the wealth of the world—and use it but as a test—of the soul strength—of the individual. It is always a—trust—given to those—who should be strong enough to use it—only—constructively—but few, very few, really pass that test under the temptation—existing in the world at large today. If we choose—we can raise the humblest of God's children—who have sufficient preparation, into wealth, power, and prominence, if by so doing, help can be given to many others—through such accomplishment."

After examining other containers filled with more jewels, we turned and re-entered the council hall. Looking toward the entrance through which we had first come, I saw my loved ones—Lotus and our son—in charge of one of the Ascended Masters—whom Saint Germain said was known as Amen Bey. After greetings had been exchanged, we were conducted to seats before—the panel on the east wall. In groups of from three to twelve came the blessed ones of the—Ascended Host—until seventy of them were seated.

A great hush fell upon all assembled, and for a few moments the silence was breathless—expectant. A ball of—soft White Light—began to form—in front of the panel—increasing rapidly in size and brilliance—until it became an oval—at least seven feet in height. As though born from within the Light itself—stepped a most Glorious Being—tall, majestic, and powerful. He made the sign uniting the finite with Infinity, and in a voice that—thrilled every atom of mind and body—asked—if all were ready.

A blazing light—flashed forth from the substance that composed the panel—until it looked like a mirror of Living Light. In a moment, this changed—into a crystal clear atmosphere—and it then became a cosmic screen upon which—living pictures—in all dimensions could be portrayed—with no limit to the space—that could be observed. It was self-evident—that everything—which had or ever could take place—in all Eternity—might be made visible on this screen—if the Directing Intelligence so desired.

The first scenes portrayed the continent of "Mu"—the activity and accomplishment of its people, and the height to which that civilization attained. This covered a period of thousands of years. Then came events that surely must have been—a reign of terror—to the inhabitants of that land. A cataclysm occurred which tore the surface of the earth—until all collapsed within itself. The ancient land of Mu sank beneath the waves—of what is now the Pacific Ocean—where it still rests wrapped in its mantle of water. Again—it will rise—and once more absorb the Life and Light of the physical sun.

Next, came the growth to beauty, wisdom, and power of Atlantis, a great continent covering a large part of what is now the Atlantic Ocean. At that time, there existed solid land between Central America and what today is Europe. The things accomplished in that age—were tremendous—but again the people's misuse—of the Mighty God Energy—overwhelmed them and, as things were thrown more and more out of balance—the tearing apart of the earth's surface by cataclysmic action was re-experienced.

It left but a small remnant of Atlantis—merely an island in mid-ocean—cut off from close contact with the rest of the civilized world. The east and west portions of the land had sunk beneath the Atlantic Ocean—leaving only the island called Poseidonis. It had been the heart of the then known civilized world, and preparation was made—to protect and preserve—its most important activities—as a central focus—to carry forward certain unfinished work. In that period very great attainment was reached both—spiritually and materially.

The mechanical development of this cycle reached a very high state of achievement, and one of its most remarkable expressions was the perfection of their aerial navigation. The air-transportation of our modern life is—as yet—very crude and primitive—compared to what was then on Atlantis. The Great Masters of Light and Wisdom—made this possible—for the people of Poseidonis because they inspired, instructed, protected, and revealed knowledge of great advancement—in every phase of human activity.

A large portion of these people became aware of the—Great Inner God Power—within the individual but as before—the human side of their nature or outer activities again usurped—the Great Energy. Selfishness and misuse of this transcendent wisdom and power gained the ascendency to even greater height than before. The Masters of the Ancient Wisdom—saw the people were building another destructive momentum—and that a third cataclysm was threatening. They warned the inhabitants—again and again as previously—but only those who served the "Light" gave heed.

Great buildings were constructed—of imperishable material—where records were placed—that have been preserved through the centuries. These remain in a state of perfect preservation—now—on the bed of the Atlantic Ocean—hermetically sealed. They will be brought to the light of day—by the Great Ones—who directed their preparation—and control their protection.

In them are recorded humanity's advance and accomplishment of that period, so there has been no permanent loss to mankind of the activities of the Atlantean civilization. Beside the preserving of such records, great wealth, principally gold and jewels, was transferred at that time to other points of safety. This has been and will continue to be guarded over the centuries—and used at a future time for the uplift and advancement of generations—yet unborn.

The final cataclysm spent its momentum, and the last remaining fragment of a once world-empire sank to rest—for purification through the centuries—beneath the present Atlantic Ocean. The remembrance of Atlantis and her people, unlike the lost continent of Mu, has not been entirely forgotten or obliterated in the history of mankind—for it has been recorded in many ways through the centuries. Even though twelve thousand years have elapsed since the sinking, fragments of information concerning it—still drift to us from most unexpected channels. Myths and legends abound in reference to Atlantis and—these are two avenues—which preserve to mankind—certain actual conditions—that have been upon the earth—in one age or another. As time goes on indisputable proof—of its existence and the height of its attainment—will be revealed by oceanography, geology, and other scientific data.

Then passed before our vision the ancient civilizations—of the Gobi and Sahara Deserts—showing the rise and fall of their principal activities. The decline in each of these was due this time—not to cataclysmic action—but to being overrun by hordes of primitive souls—taking embodiment in that cycle.

Next came pictures of Egypt—her rise and fall—the latter being due to the deliberate misuse of knowledge and power—by a large number of the humanity embodied in that land—whose predominant qualities—were pride of their intellectual accomplishments—and rebellion against the restraint—of their lower nature.

Egypt rose to her greatest height—by the right use of knowledge and power. These always demand humility—obedience of the intellect to the God-Self Within—absolute and unconditional control—of the human or lower nature—in those who seek such gifts—if they are to avoid destruction. The souls embodied in Egypt—during her decline—were not undeveloped—as were those in the civilizations of the Gobi and Sahara Deserts. On the contrary, they had attained the conscious use of knowledge and power, and—deliberately—chose to misuse it. This activity has nothing whatsoever to do with—Wisdom—for those who are the Eternal Inheritors of the gifts from that Divine Goddess—must forever be past—all—temptation to misuse knowledge and power. Wisdom—is the right use of all that manifests—and he, who realizes this self-evident, Immutable Truth becomes an open door to all good that abides in creation.

The reference to Egypt—as a land of darkness—is most unjust for out of Egypt in her earlier cycle came—Very Great Light, and out of Egypt will again come—Very Great Light.

The next scene portrayed the rise and fall of the Roman Empire. When the darkness and degradation of those centuries had reached their lowest point—lo! Jesus appeared—pouring out His Blazing Light and Love as the Christ—and through His Transfiguration, Resurrection, and Ascension—such an overwhelming flood of—God's Perfection—spread over the earth—that never again can so vast a darkness encompass humanity—in any age. The accomplishment—of His Life—stands Eternally Recorded—upon the atmosphere of this planet—and acts as a magnet—drawing mankind unto—a Like Perfection.

The coming of Jesus was—an initiation—to the people of our world and—a Cosmic Command—to use the Power of Divine Love—in all their future activities. This outpouring—of His Love—to the earth—at its darkest cycle—became the birth of the Christ Child in the individual. He called forth—once again—the Cosmic, Divine, Blue Print—and revealed the Decree for the incoming age. That plan is Complete Dominion over all things finite through the Full Stature of the Christ Within every human being.

Next, came the reign of Richard the Lion Heart of England. Humanity has little or no knowledge of the real, spiritual activity that took place—during those years. The same Light that inspired Richard's enthusiasm and activities in the crusades, released—through his followers and the people of that time—certain forces—that the Ascended Host used at Inner levels of consciousness.

Then, came pictures of the recent world war in Europe and these disclosed the activities—that generated it. Only a few individuals—know the real cause—and no doubt it is for the best—more do not. It is too destructive—for the consciousness to contemplate. Nothing can possibly be gained by focusing—the attention upon war. This too perhaps was the reason why the period from Richard to the world war was not portrayed. Here, the activities of the Ascended Host were revealed—and we saw them dissolve—the cause and greater part—of the accumulated momentum of the world's recent conflict.

They accomplished it—by consciously focusing and directing—enormous—Rays of Light—whose power to consume and transmute is—too stupendous—for finite description. These Perfected Ones have been watching for the Cosmic Moment to arrive when they might perform for humanity a

Service of Love that has been long awaited and of which mankind has as yet—little or no comprehension.

These remarkable pictures continued and—revealed activities stretching forth into the far future—and affecting the whole earth. They showed—many changes to come—in the surface of the land itself. One of the most important of these—concerned the progress of North America. The Divine Plan—for the future of North America—is a condition of intense activity in the greatest peace, beauty, success, prosperity, spiritual illumination, and dominion. She is to carry—the Christ Light—and—"Be"—the Guide for the rest of the earth—because America is to be the heart center of the—"Golden Age"—that is now dimly touching our horizon. The greater portion of the land of North America will stand for a very long time. This has been known for thousands of years—yes—for over two hundred thousand.

The pictures continued for nearly three hours—portraying many scenes and activities that have entirely escaped the recording of historians—and the world of science—because of their great antiquity. Wonderful and beautiful—as our moving pictures are today—they are mere toys—when compared with the living, breathing, actual existence—revealed upon this cosmic screen. Here, it was possible to watch—the Cosmic Cause—go forth of many events and conditions found upon earth—so that those watching—received instruction of most extraordinary magnitude.

At the close of the instruction, Saint Germain presented us—to the Great Ascended Master—Lanto—who had manifested from within—the Blazing Light—and then to the seventy Masters assembled.

"We shall rejoice indeed," said Lanto, turning toward us, "when you are again ready—to join in the conscious service of the glorious work at hand. This opportunity comes to you through the mighty victories—you have won over the human self and outer world. The time is nearing—when you shall be privileged—to see how truly great those victories are. Each day accept in its—Fulness—the Mighty Active 'Presence' of the Great God within you—and there can exist no such thing as failure—anywhere along the path. Everyone, who sincerely seeks the—'Light'—is always known to the Ascended Masters. On New Year's eve, we will meet here again—when there will be twelve guests from Venus. It is our wish that you be present. Saint Germain and Amen Bey will be—your sponsors."

At a signal, all became silent and received Lanto's blessing of love before returning to their respective fields of service. Most of them simply disappeared from the room within a few moments, and the rest—left by the way of the tube.

"My children, I see you are unaware of time. It is now three o'clock in the morning," remarked Saint Germain, as he turned to say, good-bye—to [paragraph continues]Lotus and our son who—after embracing me left by way of the outer reception room—as we passed through the first door on the right. "There is one thing more," he continued, "I want you to see before we go.

"Here is a group of most unusual musical instruments—that are used for a special purpose—being constructed or created so as to have a tone of special quality—for the work we do." Here, he turned to an organ key-board, and went on explaining.

"This seems to be a pipeless organ but the pipes, which are much smaller than ordinary, are placed within the case. The tone of the whole instrument is—superior to anything the earth has ever known before in music. These organs will come into use in the outer work as the incoming—Golden Age—moves forward."

Next, we examined four magnificent harps—slightly larger than those in ordinary use in the musical world today. Saint Germain seated himself at one of these and played several chords—to give me some idea of their tone. It was the most wonderful music, I have ever heard.

"This harp is a surprise for our Beloved Lotus," he said, "for on New Year's eve in this retreat—you shall hear the organ and four harps played by skilled artists." We finished the inspection of the room, and left through the door on the northwest wall.

Instead of passing out of the retreat, as we had come in, Saint Germain opened a small door on the left and entered—a glistening tunnel—whose walls sparkled with a crystal-like formation—which became instantly—illumined-by the White Light—that he always released by manipulating the electronic substance about him. We walked rapidly forward in the tunnel—came to a bronze door that opened at his touch—and stood again under the starlit sky.

We remained in perfect silence for an instant—then rising to some five hundred feet above the ground level—passed swiftly through the air and a few moments later stood beside my physical body—on the southern slope of Mount Shasta—where the panther still guarded. I had been away twenty-two hours—and as I looked up—dawn was just creeping over the eastern horizon.

"Here is your breakfast," announced Saint Germain, as he handed me—the Crystal Cup—containing a clear, white, sparkling liquid. "This is both strengthening and refreshing—so you will enjoy hiking home—because your body needs the exertion and activity. I sense something in your mind which is not at ease or at least is not clear to your consciousness."

"Yes," I replied. "I have a question that has been holding my attention for some time, and it is concerning—visualization. What is true visualization and what happens—when one does visualize?"

"True visualization," he answered, "is God's attribute and Power of Sight—acting in the mind of man. When one consciously pictures in his mind a desire he wishes fulfilled—he is using one of the most powerful means of bringing it into his visible, tangible experience. There is much confusion and uncertainty in the minds of many, concerning what actually happens—when one visualizes or makes a mental picture—of something he desires. No form ever came into existence—anywhere in the universe—unless some one had consciously held a picture of that form in his thought—for every thought contains a picture of the idea within it. Even an abstract thought has a picture of some kind—or at least a picture—that is one's mental concept of it.

"I will give you an exercise by which one may develop, consciously control, and direct his visualizing activities for definite accomplishment. There are several steps to the process—which every student can use at any and all times. The practice does bring visible, tangible results—when really applied. The first step—is to determine upon a definite plan or desire to be fulfilled. In this, see that it is constructive, honorable, and worthy of your time and effort. Be sure to examine your—motive—for bringing such a creation into expression. It must be honest—both toward yourself and the rest of the world, not merely to follow a whim or gratify—appetites of the physical senses. Remember there is a vast difference between use, desire, and appetite. Use—is the fulfilling of the Great Universal Law of Service. Desire—is the expanding activity of—God—through which manifestation is constantly sustained and is Perfection—enlarging itself. Appetite—is but habit—established by the continued gratification of the feeling nature—and is but energy—focused and qualified by suggestions—from the outer activity of life.

"Be—very sure—that there is no lurking feeling within—that you would be glad to benefit at the expense of another. A Real student—and only such a one will get the benefit out of this kind of training—takes the reins into his own hands and—determines—to discipline and consciously control—the human self. He chooses what shall or shall not be in his world and—through the process of picturing within his mind—designs and brings into manifestation—a definitely determined plan of Life.

"The second step—is to state your plan in words—as concise and clear as possible. Write this down. Thus, you make a record of your desire in the outer, visible, tangible world. The third step—is to close the eyes and—see—within your mind a mental picture of your desire or plan—in its finished, perfect condition and activity.

"Contemplate the fact—that your ability to create and see a picture within your own consciousness—is God's attribute of sight—acting in you. The activity of—seeing—and the power to—create—are attributes of your—God Self—which you know and feel is within you at all times. God's Life and Power are acting within your consciousness to propel into your outer world, the picture you are—seeing and feeling—within yourself.

"Keep reminding the intellect—that the ability to picture is an attribute of God—the attribute of sight. The power to feel, experience, and associate with the perfected picture is God's power. The substance used in the world without—to make the forms in your picture and plan is God's pure substance.

Then you must—know—God is the Doer, the Doing, and the Deed of every constructive form and action that ever has been sent forth—into the world of manifestation. When you thus use all the constructive processes—it is impossible for your plan—not—to come into your visible world.

"Read your desire or plan over, as many times in the day as possible and always just before retiring—because on going to sleep—immediately after contemplating the picture in your own mind—a full impression is left upon the human consciousness undisturbed—for a number of hours—enabling it to be recorded deeply in the outer activity—and allowing the force to be generated and accumulated—which propels it into the outer experience Life. In this way, you can carry any desire or picture into your consciousness—as it enters—the Great Silence—in sleep. There—it becomes charged by God's Greatest Power and Activity—which is always within—the Heart of the Great Silence.

"Under no circumstances—discuss either your desire or the fact that you are visualizing—with anyone whatsoever. This is imperative. Do not talk to yourself about it out loud—or even in a whisper—for you should realize that the greater the accumulation of energy—generated by your visualization, contemplation, and feeling the Reality of your picture—the quicker it will come—into your outer experience.

"Thousands of desires, ambitions, or ideals would have manifested into the outer experience of individuals—if they had not discussed them with friends or acquaintances. When you decide to definitely bring about an experience—through consciously directed visualization—you become The Law—God—the Law of the 'One'—and to whom there is no opposite. You must make your own decision—and stand back of your own decree—with all your power. It means you must take an unshakable, determined stand. To do so, know and feel that it is God desiring, God feeling, God knowing, God manifesting and God controlling everything concerning it. This is the Law of the 'One'—God—and God only. Until this is fully understood, you cannot and never will get your manifestation—for the moment a human element enters—you are taking it out of God's hands—and of course it cannot express—because you are neutralizing it—by the human qualities of time, space, place and a thousand and one other imaginary conditions—which God knows nothing about.

"No one can ever know God—as long as he considers—a force—opposed to God—for whenever he acknowledges that two forces can act, he has a resultant quality of neutralizing activity. When you have neutralization—you have no definite quality either way. You merely have nothing or—no thing—in your manifestation. When you acknowledge God—The One—you have only Perfection manifesting—instantly—for there is nothing to oppose or neutralize it—no element of time. So is it—established unto you—for there is none to oppose—what God decrees.

"Conditions can never improve for anyone until he desires—Perfection—and stops acknowledging—a power opposed to God—or that there is something either in or outside of him—that can prevent God's Perfection from expressing. One's very acknowledgment of a condition—that is less than all of God—is his deliberate choice of an imperfection and—that kind of choice—is the fall of man. This is—deliberate and intentional—because he is free—every moment—to think whatsoever he chooses to think. Incidentally—it takes no more energy to think a thought or picture of Perfection—than it does one of imperfection.

"You are The Creator—localized—to design and create—Perfection in your world and place—in the Universe. If Perfection and Dominion are to be expressed—you must know and acknowledge only—The Law of—'The One.' The One—exists and controls completely everywhere in the Universe. You are the Self-Consciousness of Life—The One Supreme 'Presence' of the Great Flame of Love and Light. You alone are the—Chooser—the Decreer—of the qualities and forms you wish to pour your Life into, for you are the only energizer of your world and—all it contains. When you think or feel—part of your Life energy goes forth to sustain your creation.

"Cast out of mind then, all doubt or fear of the fulfillment of that—which you are picturing. Should any such thoughts or feelings—which are after all but human emanations, thoughts and feelings that do not contain perfection, come to your consciousness instantly replace them by the full acknowledgment of your self and world as—the Life of God—'The One.' Further than that, be completely unconcerned about it—except during the time you are visualizing. Have no set time in your mind for results—except to know there is only—now—just the immediate moment. Take this discipline—use it—and you can manifest a resistless power in action—that cannot and never did fail.

"Always remember you are God picturing. You are God Intelligence directing. You are God Power propelling. It is God's—Your Substance—being acted upon. As you realize this and contemplate the fulness of it often—everything in the Universe rushes to fulfill your desire, your command, your picture—for it is all constructive and therefore—agrees with the Original Divine Plan for Self-Conscious Life. If the human side of us really agrees to the Divine Plan and accepts it—there can be no such thing as delay or failure—for all energy has the inherent quality of—Perfection—within it and rushes to serve its Creator.

"As your desire or picture is constructive—you are God seeing His Own Plan. When God Sees—it is an irrevocable decree or command—to appear Now. In the creation of this earth and system of worlds, God said—'Let there be Light'—and Light appeared. It did not take aeons of time to create—Light. The same Mighty God is in you—now—and when you see or speak—it is His attribute of sight and speech—which is acting in and through you.

"If you realize what this truly means—you can command by His Full Power and Authority—for you are His Life-Consciousness—and it is only the Self-Consciousness of your Life—that can command, picture, or desire a constructive and Perfect Plan. Every constructive plan is His Plan. Therefore, you know God is acting, commanding—'Let this desire or plan be fulfilled now'—and It is Done."

Here, Saint Germain finished speaking, and bidding me a smiling—"good-bye"—for the time being, disappeared from my sight. I turned my footsteps toward home, and the panther trotted close by my side. He had been fully twenty-four hours without food, and it was not long until he dashed off through the woods and disappeared in the heavy timber. I continued on my way and arrived home at eleven o'clock, spending the rest of the day trying to realize—the full import of what I had been privileged to experience—and how the entire concept of my world had changed so unexpectedly.

CHAPTER - IV

Mysteries of the Yellowstone

SEVEN days passed—it was then the first week in September. On the evening of the eighth day, I sat contemplating Life and its infinite expressions, when my thought turned naturally to Saint Germain. Immediately—an overwhelming love went out to him in deep gratitude for all I had been privileged to experience—through his assistance and Light.

A feeling as of a "Presence" in the room began to come over me like a breath and looking up suddenly—there he stood smiling and radiant, the very "Presence of Divinity."

"My son," he said, "am I so unexpected a visitor—that I surprise you? Surely, you know quite well that—when thinking of me—you are in contact with me, and when I think of you—I am with you. In meditation, your attention was upon me and so—I appear. Is that not according to the Law? Then, why not accept it—as natural? What one thinks upon—he draws unto himself.

"Allow me to suggest that you train yourself—never to be surprised, disappointed, or your feelings hurt under any circumstances—for perfect self-control—of all the forces within you at all times—is Dominion—and that is the reward for those who tread the pathway of 'Light' and correction of the human self.

"Remember always—that the right to command—which is Dominion—is only—permanently—retained by those—who have first learned to—obey—because he, who has learned obedience to the 'Law of The One,' becomes a Being of Cause—only—and that Cause—Love. Thus, he in—Reality—becomes 'The Law of The One'—through the quality of similarity. Watch, so nothing goes out from you except that which is harmonious, and do not allow a destructive word to pass your lips—even in jest. Remember—you deal with a force of some kind—every instant—of Eternity, and you are its qualifier at all times.

"I have come to take you on an important journey. We will be gone thirty-six hours. Draw the curtains to your room, lock the doors, and leave your body in bed. It will be guarded until our return. You have made certain Inner advancement, and a very interesting, delightful experience and journey are ahead of you."

I prepared my body for bed and soon became very still. A moment later—I stood upon the floor outside of my body—clothed in the same—golden garment—I had worn on my visit to the Royal Teton. The sense of density one has about the walls was gone—and as I passed through them—the feeling was that which one experiences—when walking through a heavy fog.

This time, I was clearly conscious of passing through space. I did not ask—where we were going but it was not long until—we came to the Royal Teton. Toward the east, stood the towering Rockies, and beyond them stretched vast plains that will one day be teeming with semi-tropical vegetation, and its people living in peace and abundance.

To the west, we could see the Sierra and Cascade mountains and still farther on the Coast Range—whose shore line is all to be changed. Northward, we looked down upon the "Yellowstone" whose marvelous beauty veils its ancient mysteries and wonders from our present American civilization.

"The word—'Yellowstone,' explained Saint Germain, "has been brought down through the centuries—for more than fourteen thousand years. At that time—the civilization of Poseidonis had reached a very high point of attainment because—a Great Master of Light was at the head of the Government. It was only during the last—five hundred years—that the decline took place, and the misuse of her great wisdom held sway. Within the present boundaries of the—Yellowstone—which are still the same, existed the richest gold mine the world has ever known. It belonged to the government and much of its wealth was used for experimental and research purposes in chemistry, invention, and science.

"Thirty-seven miles from this place, was located a—diamond mine. The stones taken from it were the most beautiful—yellow diamonds—that have ever been found within this earth—before or since that period. Among the gems which came from that mine—were a few rare stones of very remarkable beauty and perfection. If properly cut, they showed—a tiny blue flame—at the center—that looked like liquid Light. When worn by certain individuals—the radiance from this flame—could be seen more than—an inch above the surface of the stone.

"These were held sacred and—only used in the highest—most secret rites of the Ascended Masters. Sixteen of them are still held in sacred trust by the 'Brotherhood of the Royal Teton,' and will again be brought into use at an appointed time. It was because of these magnificent yellow diamonds—that the present name—Yellowstone—has come down to us.

"You, my son, were the discoverer of both mines. I will reveal the records—that are the physical evidence of what I have just been telling you. These records give the date of their discovery—amount of wealth taken out—length of time operated—description of the machinery used, which handled refractory ores recovering eighty-seven per cent of their value running of it into bullion while yet in the mine, making unnecessary any operation at the surface—where shipped—and the date of closing and sealing. Here are the duplicate records.

"In the life on Poseidonis—you lived in a beautiful home with a sister—who is now Lotus. Both attained and maintained close contact with the 'Inner God-Self'—so God was truly in action at all times. You were an official in the bureau of mines and through that connection, invented and built a wonderful airship. In it you travelled a great deal over the mountains. One day while in deep meditation, you were shown the location of these mines which you later discovered, opened up, and turned over to the government. With this explanation, I will now show you—proof—of what I have described—although there is not a trace of these mines on the surface today. Come, we will enter the mine itself."

Leaving the Royal Teton, I was perfectly conscious of passing through space and moving rapidly, until we reached a certain spot in—Yellowstone Park. Here—we descended and stood before a wall of solid rock.

"Do you see any way to enter?" asked Saint Germain, turning to me.

"No, but I feel the opening is here," I answered, as I pointed to a certain spot on the granite wall. He smiled, and going up to the place indicated, laid his hand upon it and in a moment we stood before a metal door—unsealed.

"You see," he explained, "we have our own methods of sealing any entrance we choose—for protection—and it is impossible for it ever to be found or entered unless—we so desire. The substance with which we hermetically seal places and things is drawn—from the universal. It is harder than the rock itself—though in appearance—exactly like it.

"In this way—we are able to protect entrances to retreats, buildings, buried cities, mines and secret chambers of—the Great Ascended Brotherhood of Light—many of which have been held in a state of perfect preservation—for over seventy thousand years. When we no longer have use for such places or things—we return them back to the universal—so you see all power becomes the willing servitor of one—who has conquered himself. All forces of the Universe are awaiting our command, whenever it is the part of—wisdom and love—to use them."

On the door we faced, was a replica of a man's right hand—raised in the metal itself—at about the level of my shoulder. It looked strikingly like my present physical hand.

"Place your hand over this metal one," said Saint Germain, "and press hard." I obeyed. It fitted over the other perfectly. I pressed with all my strength. Slowly, the great door opened and he continued:

"You have retained that form and size of hand for several embodiments. It was placed on the door by the government—as an honor—because you were the discoverer of the mine. That hand is a model—of your hand—fourteen thousand years ago."

We entered through this door, and passed into a long round tunnel—finally emerging into a great cavity. There to my utter amazement—I found tools and machinery of various kinds—made of an imperishable white metal—in as perfect a state of preservation—as if constructed but yesterday. In the center of the cavity, was a shaft. Our present mining engineers would be amazed—at the simplicity and perfection—of the mining activities of that former age. The same method will again be brought forth into use—here in America—within the next century.

Saint Germain stepped to the shaft and pulled a lever. Soon a cage of peculiar design came to the top. We stepped inside, and he touched a smaller lever within it. As we began moving downward toward the two hundred foot level, we came to a station. Continuing on down to the seven hundred foot level, we stopped. This was the central station, and from it led five tunnels—like the spokes of a wheel.

These were all perfectly round and lined with the same white metal of which the machinery was constructed. It was so thick and strong—that only the collapse of the mountain itself—could crush it. Two of the five tunnels were driven into the mountain for more than two thousand feet. In the central station was one engine—that handled all the cars.

"The white metal you see," explained Saint Germain, "is a most remarkable discovery—for it is light in weight, tougher than anything known, untarnishable, and imperishable. You may only give a fragmentary description of all these marvels—that are actual physical proof of the great height of this ancient civilization. Such wonders have existed and are now—in your midst—undreamed of until this revelation shall go forth." As we came to the end of the tunnel, he showed me the drills—that had been used in that distant day. "These drills," he continued, "sent forth a tube of blue-white flame about an inch in diameter. They operated at amazing speed—consuming the rock as they passed through."

We returned to the station, and entered a triangular-shaped room between two tunnels. At the far end, were containers made of the same white metal. They were about twelve inches square and three feet in length. Saint Germain opened one and—showed me the wonderful, uncut, yellow diamonds. I was speechless, they were so beautiful. I think—I hear my readers say—"Do you mean to tell me that these were physical?" To that perfectly natural question, I wish to answer—yes—just as physical—as the diamonds you wear on your fingers today. Other containers were filled with cut stones of fabulous value.

We then returned to the entrance of the mine. Saint Germain closed the door and—sealed it as before. No one not—an Ascended Master—could have distinguished it from the surrounding rock. Rising from the ground, we quickly covered the thirty-seven miles—to the gold mine. This time, we stood on the very top of the mountain—near a cone shaped rock—that looked perfectly solid. It was about fifteen feet in diameter at the base and perhaps ten feet in height.

"Watch—closely," he said, as he laid his hand against it. Slowly a triangular shaped section moved out—disclosing a flight of steps leading downward. We descended these stairs for some distance—and soon came to a cavity at the top of a shaft—similar to the one in the diamond mine.

"You will notice the absence of crushers," he continued, "everything is done within the mine itself. Not a thing is handled at the surface." We stopped at the four hundred foot level where there was another—immense cavity. Here—complete equipment—for treating the ore was located. He explained the extreme simplicity of the process used—which seemed incredible—it was so simple.

We continued on down—to the eight hundred foot level—and saw the same arrangement—as in the diamond mine. Here again, were tunnels going out from a central point, like the spokes of a wheel. Three triangular-shaped rooms—had been built between these tunnels, containing the remaining output from the mine—just before it had been closed. The same white metal containers were here—as in the other rooms. Only three of them—am I allowed to describe.

The first receptacle contained nuggets—from an ancient river bed—in a placer formation—at the eight hundred foot level—in which the gravel had been slightly cemented together—holding the gold. This condition existed—for a depth of twelve hundred feet—and held immense value. The second container was filled—with wire gold—from a white quartz vein—at the four hundred foot level. Another—held solid gold discs—weighing eight pounds each.

"The place in which they stored all the gold," he explained, "was known—as the bullion room. There have been—duplicate records—kept of this mine. The originals being in the record room—at the retreat in the Royal Teton—and the duplicates here." We returned to the surface. Again Saint Germain sealed the entrance as described and turning to me again, said:

"My son, you discovered these mines and—assisted by your colleagues, put them into operation—and brought about this perfection. You also made the records—on the imperishable metal—which I will show you in the Royal Teton. The Ascended Masters—saw that the cataclysm of twelve thousand years ago was approaching—and knowing the mines would not be much affected—had them prepared and sealed—for use in a far distant age—into which we have now entered.

"At seven different periods of your many embodiments—the memory and process—for making these records—has been recalled. You will bring them forth again—in the present age to—the blessing of all mankind. This accounts for your feeling since childhood—of interest in ancient records of all kinds—and that you would have much to do with such work again in this life.

"Come, we will now return to the Royal Teton. There—in a room adjoining the great audience hall—are these records—to which I have referred. It is a place for the preservation of inventions and scientific discoveries. The one we were in on our former visit—contained only records of the various civilizations."

We returned to the retreat, and entered this time by way of the tube, as on our first visit. Stepping out, we passed through the second door to the right of the entrance. It opened directly into—the scientific record room—a space about seventy, by forty, by fifteen feet. The entire walls, ceiling, and floor were lined with the same—imperishable white metal—of which the shelving and containers were constructed.

Saint Germain drew out one of the latter and handed me the record—I had made of the diamond mine. Again, I was able to read it—but this time—he told me to call upon the God-Self Within—and thus let—It—reveal the complete former knowledge which I had at that time. The record gave a clear but condensed history of the discovery and operation. He handed me another spindle, and on it was—the complete history of the gold mine.

"Now—that you have seen the physical proof of what I have explained," he said, "I want you to know that—I will never tell you anything—which I cannot prove." Here he turned toward me with a—piercing look—in his eyes that—passed clear through—my mind and body.

"My son," he continued, "you have done well and are calm and poised under these recent experiences. Much depends upon your next step. Focus your entire attention upon—the All-Controlling God-Self Within you—and do not forget to hold it there."

In the light of what occurred later, it was well—he had fortified me with that admonition. With that warning, he led the way across the large audience hall—to the great bronze door on the west wall. Placing his hand against it, the panel slowly moved upward until we had entered, and then closed after us. I stopped—immovable—with amazement, for I looked upon—that—which human eyes are—rarely if ever—permitted to behold; and the scene held me motionless—so great was the fascination of its beauty and wonder.

About twelve feet in front of me, stood a block of snow white onyx—three feet high and sixteen inches square. On this rested a—crystal sphere—filled with a ceaselessly moving, colorless—"Light"—in which were points of radiance—darting to and fro. The sphere continually sent forth—rays of prismatic colors—to a distance of about six inches. It seemed made of—living substance—so constantly did it scintillate.

Out of the top of the crystal ball poured forth three—Plumes of Flame—one molten gold, one rose pink, and the other electric blue—extending at least three feet in height. Near the top, each section—bent over like an ostrich plume—graceful, beautiful, and in—perpetual motion. The—radiance—from this gorgeous sphere filled the entire chamber—producing a sensation of electronic energy—no words can convey. The Light, Life, and beauty of that scene simply—overwhelm—human powers of description.

We stepped toward the far end of the room, and there, side by side, stood—three crystal caskets—each containing a human body. As I came nearer—my heart almost stopped beating—for within were the forms Lotus, our son, and I had used—in an ancient embodiment. I recognized them readily—for Lotus still retains some resemblance to that body—but the bodies of our son and myself had features of greater regularity and perfect physiques. All showed—the full perfection—of a type almost like that of the ancient Greek.

They looked as—life-like—as though only sleeping. Each had wavy golden hair and was clothed in garments of a—similar golden fabric—to that in the robes worn by the figures—in the tapestry. An Ascended Master—had but to look upon these bodies—to see registered—every vital action—experienced in any physical embodiment—since that time. Thus, they acted as—mirrors—to record passing activities—which, however, left their original perfection unchanged.

Each casket stood upon a large base made of the same kind of white onyx as that on which the sphere was placed. These were covered by lids of crystal, fitted very tightly in a groove around the edge, but were not sealed. On the cover of all three just over the center of the chest was a—seven-pointed star. Below it were—four hieroglyphics. At the end, and placed so it would be just over the top of the head, was a—six-pointed star. On the side just beneath the shoulders were—two clasped hands—and farther down nearer the feet, was a—lighted torch—placed so the—flame—touched the lid of the casket. This flame—remained golden—no matter what other colors of light played through the room. At the opposite end was a—five-pointed star—under the feet. All the emblems were—raised—as if embossed upon the crystal.

"These bodies," explained Saint Germain, "belonged to you three in one particular life, when you left the Golden City—to do a special work. Your experiences were so—terrific—and yet so much good was accomplished in that life that a—Great Cosmic Being—appeared and gave the command—to preserve them—until such time as you could—raise your bodies and—return to the Golden City. He gave full direction for their—preservation—which was faithfully carried out, as you see.

"Now, you can all realize how—important and necessary it is—to keep keenly aware of and deeply centered upon the Master Christ-Self Within—that only God's Love, Wisdom, and Perfection may act through your minds and bodies—at all times."

At that moment—a Dazzling Light and Tremendous Power surged through me and my—God Self—spoke.

"Great Master of Light—Parent, Brother, and Friend—O Mighty Son of God—Thou hast indeed an Everlasting Love and through It, thou hast attained thy well deserved Eternal Peace and Mastery over the five lower kingdoms.

The Great God Self in these children, thou lovest so well, shall soon come forth in—Full Conscious Dominion—to give every assistance thou hast so long desired—for each of God's children has a service to perform—which none but he may give. I call forth the—'Great Light'—from the very—Heart of God—to bless you forever."

As these words were spoken—a great shaft of Light blazed forth—filling the chamber with points of brilliant prismatic colors. They darted everywhere in the room and all became a blaze of rainbow Light, pulsing with Life.

"See—my Son," said Saint Germain, "how perfectly—you can let the Great God Self express Itself! You shall soon be able to do this consciously and at will—whenever you desire.

"Notice the stalactite effect on the ceiling and the—silver white—appearance of the walls. They are all made of—precipitated—substance, and the room is maintained at the same comfortable temperature at all times." We crossed to the far end of the chamber and stood before—a polished archway in the wall. Saint Germain placed his hand upon it, and a door opened disclosing the wonderful white metal—equipment—for making the records. "In the age we are now entering," he continued, "much equipment will be brought into humanity's use—that has been preserved—and so will not have to come through either the avenue of invention or discovery."

"How is it," I asked, "that everything in this retreat and the mines is kept so free from dust and the ventilation so good?"

"That," he explained, "is very simple. The Ascended Masters use the same—force—to cleanse and ventilate by which they produce heat, light, and power. The emanation from any one of them—as they pass through the mines or chambers—instantly consumes all unnecessary substance. It is nearing the second morning since leaving your body, and we must now return."

We passed through the audience chamber out of the door at the left of the tube, and stood once more under the light of the stars. We came back to my room quickly and a moment later I was again in my body. Saint Germain stood beside me holding out the familiar crystal cup, filled this time with an—amber colored liquid. I drank it, and felt the vivifying effects pass through every cell of my body.

"Now sleep as long as you can," he said and disappeared from sight. I must have slept soundly—for I awakened many hours later—completely refreshed, my body renewed in strength and power.

CHAPTER - V

Inca Memories

THE next ten days passed uneventfully. Through past training, I never went to sleep without holding my attention upon—the Great God Self Within and sending a thought of loving gratitude to Saint Germain. On the evening of the eleventh day while retiring, I heard his voice say distinctly:

"Come!" I had learned to obey that call and immediately stood outside of my body, passed quickly through space, and in a few moments came to the Royal Teton. He stood upon its side awaiting my arrival. This time, he had called me to come to where he was. I obeyed and saluted him.

"At your service," I said, stepping to his side, and smiling at me he replied:

"We have work to do. Let us go!"

I was fully aware of the direction in which we traveled—certain we were going a little west of south. Soon, we saw the lights from a city, and Saint Germain, directing my attention to them, remarked:

"Los Angeles." After traveling some distance farther on, we passed over another lighted section and this time to my inquiry, he answered:

"Mexico City." We then came to a tropical forest and began to descend. Presently we stood upon an old ruins.

"These are the ruins of the ancient temple of Mitla in the state of Oaxaca, Mexico," he explained. "You three came into embodiment to give assistance, as the Inca civilization reached its apex. With the approval of the Ascended Masters who were directing your own growth, you chose to come into the Inca family to give the service needed at that time.

"Here, you were born as the children of an Inca ruler who was a strong soul of great growth and illumination. In deep love for his people, he called to the One Supreme God for—'Light'—abundance, and perfection to bless them and the land.

"The Inca's devotion to his Source was—very great—for he knew and consciously acknowledged—the power of the—'Great Central Sun.' This True Understanding was taught to the Incan people and, because they knew to what the—Great Central Sun—referred, used the Sun as the symbol of the—Godhead. They had—Real—Inner Understanding, and acknowledged the Fulness of the power from this—Great Central Sun—which today we call the—'Christ'—for it is the—Heart—of the Christ Activity in the Universe.

"Because of the Inca ruler's devotion to both his Source and the people, his deep desire for blessing and Light to guide and help them was granted, and—fourteen—from the Golden City—over the Sahara Desert—responded to give him assistance. You, Lotus and your Son were three of that fourteen.

"When you were ten, Lotus twelve, and your Son fourteen, all were placed under my care and direction—to be prepared and trained—for the work you did later. At that time, I resided in the Golden City—but after the preliminary attunement had taken place, I came to the palace daily and gave the necessary radiation and instruction. This continued for four years—before it was revealed to your father.

"The Inca ruler was amazed at the wisdom of the children, and constantly poured out his praise and gratitude to God for thus blessing him. When you were fourteen, the same—Great Cosmic Master—who had taken us all to the Golden City at the end of the embodiment in the Sahara Civilization—appeared to the Inca and told him his petition had been granted—in a very Real manner.

"It was from this time on for over seventy years, that the Incan civilization came to its greatest height. I came daily from the time you were fourteen—instructed and attuned the Inca Ruler as well as you three. You were referred to as the Inca children from the—'Sun.' His gratitude, love and co-operation were wonderful indeed, and he was taught to understand and use the—Great Cosmic Law.

"Your childhood and youth were wonderful for no cloud came to mar the beauty of that training. Your son was taught the—Laws of Government and the—Divine Duties—of a Ruler; Lotus the Inner Work and given the Full Law and consecration of Priestess in the—'Temple of the Sun.' You were taught the Cosmic Laws of the priesthood, also secretly, the generalship of Armies.

"After ten years of special training in Peru—all three of you were sent north to one of the new colonies of the Incan Empire; for the purpose of helping the people to expand their activities and stimulate their progress. You went forth with all the love, honor, and blessing the Inca ruler knew how to give, and established the Capital of the Colony at what is now—Mitla—in the state of Oaxaca, Mexico.

"Here, you built a great temple under the direction of—Those in the Golden City—by whom you had been instructed and helped. Lotus was called—Mitla—in that life, and it was in honor of her that the city was named. Here she served as—priestess—for more than—forty years. It was one of the most magnificent temples of that period, and no expense was spared, for the secret part of it—built below the surface of the earth—was to remain, and bear witness to that splendid civilization—centuries later. You knew this at the time it was built, and certain definite orders were given and fulfilled concerning it; because the entire construction was directed—by one of the Great Ascended Masters from the Golden City.

"The outer part was made of massive stones, some of which may still be seen—today—among the ruins. The interior was lined with marble, onyx, and jade. The jade came from—a secret source—in the Andes Mountains that has never been revealed to any one. The coloring of the interior decorative work was most artistic and beautiful, the main color scheme being—gold, purple, rose and shell pink.

"The Inner Sanctuary was gold—with designs in purple and white. The chair—in which the priestess officiated—was also of gold. Here—the Spiritual Power—was focused and maintained—which radiated out to the empire and its people. With this explanation as a preliminary, we will now enter the subterranean temple—in which a room has been preserved—amidst the ruins—of a once great glory." We went some distance farther away—when Saint Germain commanded:

"Stand back!"

He focused a—Ray of Mighty Power—on a pile of great rocks before us. Suddenly—they were thrown in every direction—uncovering a cube of—rose colored granite. He stepped forward and placed his hand upon it. Slowly it turned, as if on a pivot, revealing an opening about three feet wide with well defined steps leading downward. We descended twenty-one steps to a door that seemed to be made of copper—but Saint Germain said it was—a combination of metals alloyed—so as to make it imperishable.

Pressing on a cube of rock to the right of the entrance, the door swung slowly open and admitted us into a small room. At the farther side was a great archway—closed by another massive door. This time, he pressed his foot upon a stone of peculiar design in the floor, and the door moved back—disclosing a chamber of immense proportions—that seemed very much in need of cleansing and ventilation. No sooner had the thought entered my mind—than the place became filled with—a powerful violet light—followed by a soft white haze—becoming brilliant as the noon day sun. The cleansing was complete, for everything was fresh, clean, and filled with the—fragrance of roses.

As we entered the great room, my attention was held by a number—of the most remarkable portraits—I have ever seen. They were etched on solid gold—in colors—true to life.

"These," Saint Germain explained, "are also—Indestructible. Five of them are of the Inca Ruler, Lotus, your son, you and myself—all in the likeness of the bodies we used at that time. It was only during the—Incan period—that this particular kind of art has ever been expressed. Through the devotion of—Lotus to her own God-Flame—at that time, she attracted a—Great Master from Venus—who taught her. That kind of art was different from anything known on earth—in any age. The Master from Venus—only allowed a certain number to be made—because this particular type of art was centuries ahead of its time, and therefore was not permitted to be used at that period of the world's development. However, it will come forth in the present—Golden Age we have now entered.

"My son—Oh, that the people of America could only—understand—what tremendous possibilities stand before them—waiting, waiting, waiting—for them to turn away from creeds, cults, dogmas, isms and all else that binds and limits—by keeping their attention—from the Great God 'Presence'—within their own hearts. Oh, that they might—realize—what freedom, power, and Light await their service, dependent—only—on their recognition and use of the—Great Loving 'Presence' Within—breathing through them each moment—know and feel—the Almighty Control—it has over all manifestation. Oh, could they only realize that their—bodies—are the—'Temples of the Most High Living God'—who is—Ruler—of heaven and earth; that they might know what it means—to love—that Mighty Self, talk to it, acknowledge it—in all things, and—feel—the Reality of That 'Presence'—with at least as great a certainty as they do other persons and things. If they could only—feel—the closeness and Reality of the—'Great Presence'—deeply, even for a moment, nothing could ever again stand between them and the—Same Mighty Supreme Accomplishment—as Jesus—and other Ascended Masters have attained.

"O America—Beloved Children of the 'Light'—let—this Great God 'Presence,' its wisdom and power surge through you—now—and see how quickly God's Kingdom—can and will—manifest upon earth. America is the Way Shower among the nations—bearing the—'Light'—that heralds the incoming Golden Age. Regardless of her present conditions—'That Light' shall burst forth and consume the shadows that seek to disrupt her—Ideals and Love—for the Great God Self."

We then passed through a door at the right where we found more imperishable records—this time of the Incan civilization and the important part it played in that cycle.

"You recalled the process for making these records from the memory of your life fourteen thousand years ago," remarked Saint Germain. "They will be transported to the Royal Teton together with the portraits—for this secret temple has completely fulfilled its usefulness and is—now—to be dissolved."

Soon Beautiful Glistening Beings appeared and removed the portraits and records. When they had finished, we returned to the entrance and walked some distance away. Saint Germain—focused—his attention for a few moments upon the position of the secret temple and—stood very silent. I felt a sudden stillness—grip and hold me—motionless. There was a great rumbling—like an earthquake. In a moment—all was over—and the secret temple, which had been the most magnificent creation of its day—collapsed into ruins.

I could but gasp at Saint Germain's—stupendous power. Truly—the Great Ascended Masters are—Gods. It is no wonder in the mythology of the ancients that—their activities—have been brought down to us in the guise of myth and fable. They wield Tremendous God Power at—all—times because they hold with—unwavering determination—to the Great God—"Presence"—and hence all power is given unto them—for they are—All—Perfection.

"When Jesus said, 'All these things I have done, ye shall do and even greater things shall ye do,' he knew whereof he spoke," continued Saint Germain.

"He came forth to—reveal—the Conscious Dominion and Mastery that it—is possible—for every human being to attain and express—while still here on earth. He showed the—Dominion of the Ascended Master—and—proved—to mankind that it—is—possible for everyone, to so call forth his—God Self—that he can consciously control—all—things human.

"The Great Ascended Masters of Love, Light, and Perfection—who have guided the growth of humanity on this planet from the beginning—are no figment of anyone's imagination. They are Real—visible—tangible—glorious—living—breathing—Beings—of such Love, Wisdom, and Power that the human mind—gasps—at the immensity of it. They work—everywhere—in the universe with complete freedom and limitless power, to do—naturally—all that the average individual considers—super-natural.

"They are wielders of such Power and manipulators of such Force as to stagger the imagination of the person—in the outer world. They are the—Guardians—of the race and, as in the world of physical education various grades of teachers are provided—to guide the development of the individual's growth—from childhood to maturity, and then beyond preparing him for special work; so do the—Ascended Masters of Perfection—exist to educate and help the individual that he too may grow beyond—ordinary, human expression. Thus, he develops his Super-Human Attributes, until like the student graduating from college—the one under the care and instruction of an Ascended Master—graduates out of his humanity—into the—Full—Continuous—Expression—of his Divinity.

"The Ascended Master is an individual—who by self-conscious effort—has generated enough Love and Power—within himself—to snap the chains of all human limitation, and so he stands—free and worthy—to be trusted with the use of forces—beyond—those of human experience. He; feels himself—'One'—with Omnipresent God—'Life.' Hence, all forces and things obey his command because he is a Self-Conscious Being of free will controlling all—by the manipulation of the 'Light' within—Himself.

"It is through the radiation or outpouring of this 'Light'—which is really his own—'Luminous Essence of Divine Love'—that an Ascended Master is able—to help—those who come under his care and direction.

"When such an—Outpouring—to a student takes place, his own Inner bodies—and by that I mean his emotional, mental, and Causal bodies—absorb the—Master's Luminous Essence—and the 'Light' within them glows and expands like a spark—which one fans into a—flame.

"This 'Luminous Essence' has within It the Highest Force in the Universe—for it dissolves all discord—and establishes—Perfect Balance—in all manifestation. The Ascended Master's—Body—is constantly pouring out Rays of his 'Light Essence'—upon the discords of earth—dissolving them as—the rays of force—which we call light and heat from our physical sun—dissolve a fog.

"The Radiation—they pour out to humanity of earth is—Consciously Drawn Energy to which they give—quality—and again send it out to accomplish a—definite result. In this way, they give protection thousands and thousands of times to persons, places, conditions, and things of which mankind is totally oblivious, going on its appointed way—serenely unconscious—of its Protectors and Benefactors.

"In this kind of activity—the Ascended Masters—are able to change the bodies they function in—like one ordinarily changes his clothes—for the cellular structure is always under conscious control, and—every atom—is obedient to their slightest direction. They are free to use one or more bodies, if the work they desire to do requires it, for their—ability—to assemble or dissolve an atomic body—is absolutely—Unlimited. They are All-Powerful Manifestors—of All Substance and Energy for the forces in Nature—which mean the four elements—are their willing and obedient servants.

"These Glorious Beings—who guard and help the evolving human race, are called the Ascended Masters of Love, Light, and Perfection. They are all the word—Master—implies because—by bringing forth the Love, Wisdom, and Power of the God Self Within—they manifest their—Mastery—over all that is human. Hence, they have—'Ascended'—into the next expression above the human—which is the Super-human—Divinity—Pure and Eternally, All-Powerful 'Perfection.'

"The humanity of earth frequently, in its ignorance and limitation, presumes to pass judgment upon and express various opinions about Jesus and many others of the Ascended Host. That practice is one of the most binding things it can indulge in, for in such activity—the criticism and judgment sent forth in this way simply return—to its generator—and thus mankind is bound more tightly to its self-created suffering and limitation. The activity of the Law is that—the Ascended Masters—having freed themselves from human limitations—have become a—Blazing Outpouring of Light—into which—no human thought of discord can possibly enter. This compels all destructive—thought creation and feeling—to return to its sender and—bind him—still more closely in the chains of his own creation.

"If human beings could see their own thoughts, feelings, and words go out into the atmosphere—upon the ethers—gather and gather more of their kind and return—they would not only be amazed at what they give birth to—but would scream for deliverance—and if for no other reason than to blot such creation out of mind—they would with full determination—face their own Divinity—and enter into it. Thoughts and feelings—are—living—pulsating—things. The individual who—knows that—will use his wisdom—and control himself—accordingly.

"Jesus is to mankind gaining its experience on this earth—as the Great God Self—within every human being—is to the personal or outer self. He—revealed the—Master Record—to the outer world, and—He—is still the—Living Proof—of the individual's ability to free himself from—all—limitation and to express Divinity—as was originally intended—for the first condition in which humanity existed was—wholly harmonious and free.

"When some of those individuals—who study Life and the Laws of the Universe, more deeply than the mass of earth's children—become aware of the fact that there are Ascended Masters—they often desire to go to these Great Ones for instruction. While, in many instances, this is an unconscious upreaching of the soul within to the—Greater Light—yet the personal self little realizes in what relation it stands to those—Great Beings—who are Wholly Divine.

"There is a way by which an intensely earnest and determined student may make contact with one of them but that can only be through the activity of enough Love and discipline of the personality. If the motive for such contact be for the gratification of curiosity thinking to prove or disprove the Ascended Masters' existence—to merely solve a problem—or to convince a doubt in the personality—it will never come about—rest assured of that—for the Ascended Host are never concerned with satisfying the—human side—of any student. Their entire effort is with the—expansion of the God Self Within—so that Its Power may be released forcefully enough—to snap the limitations in the human self that do not give it a Perfect Vehicle for use in the mental, emotional, and physical worlds of manifestation. These are the realms of thought, feeling, and action.

"Human weaknesses and limitation simply impair the vehicle—that should be trained and kept in the best possible condition—as an efficient servant—for the use of the Great Inner God Self. The human body with its faculties—is—God's Temple of Energy—which the 'Great God Presence' provides—and through this outer self—It wishes to express a Perfect Divine Plan or Design. If the uncontrolled sense appetites—and demands of the personality—waste the God energy—so the 'Inner Presence' is not given command of the vehicle—It steadily withdraws—the human self loses the power to manipulate mind and body—and the temple collapses into decrepitude and dissolution. We then have the condition the world calls death.

"The person—who seeks to contact an Arisen Master—in the visible, tangible, living, breathing body without the preparation needed—to gradually attune his own outer structure and mind—is in the same position a child in kindergarten would be—were he to see a college professor and insist on learning the A. B. C's under him.

"The Ascended Masters are—Really—Great Batteries of Tremendous Power and Energy and whatever touches their—Radiance—becomes highly charged with their—'Light Essence'—through the same activity—that makes a needle—kept in contact with a magnet—take on its qualities—and become a magnet also. All their help and Radiation is forever a free gift of Love. This is the reason they—never—use any of their force to compel.

"The Law of Love—the Law of the Universe—and the Law of the individual—does not permit the Ascended Master to interfere—with the free will of the individual—except at those periods of Cosmic Activity—in which the Cosmic Cycle supersedes that of the—individual. It is during these times—the Ascended Master may give—more—than ordinary assistance. The earth has entered such a Cycle now, and the greatest Outpouring of the—'Light'—the earth has ever known is being and will continue to be shed upon humanity—to purify it and re-establish the Order and Love that is—imperative—for the future maintenance of our planet and the system of worlds to which we belong. All that does not—or will not—come into the action of Order—Balance—Peace—must of necessity pass into some other school-room of the universe—and work out its own understanding of this Law—in some other way—than is to be the expression of the future Life upon our earth.

"There is only one passport into the 'Presence,' of these—Great Ones—and that is—Enough Love—poured out to one's own—God Self—and to—Them—united with the determination to root out of the human all discord and selfishness. When an individual becomes determined—enough—to serve only the Constructive Plan of Life, he disciplines—perfectly—his human nature, no matter how unpleasant the task. Then he will automatically draw to himself the attention of an—Ascended Master—who will take note of his struggles and pour out courage, strength, and Love—sustaining him—until he maintains—permanent contact—with the Inner God Self.

"The Ascended Master knows and sees all concerning the student—for he reads clearly the record—which the student has made in his own aura. This reveals the state of the disciple's development—his strength as well as his weakness. The Ascended Master—is—the All-Knowing Mind and the All-Seeing Eye of God—for from him—nothing—can be hidden. The one who wishes to come into the visible, tangible—'Presence'—of the Ascended Host—should understand that unless he makes himself a Radiating Sun of Love, Light, and Perfection—which the Master can expand, and use as a part of Himself—that he can direct to any place consciously at will—he would be useless—merely a barnacle and drain upon the Master's work and world.

"If the student has not, be not willing to, or does not discipline the personal self—so it is calm in mind—peaceful and loving in feeling—and strong in body—he is not material that the Ascended Master can use in the—more-than-human work that he does. When the student has not a strong, controlled, well developed vehicle—he is unable to co-operate with an Ascended Master, and thus do—work—of a kind which is beyond that—of the ordinary human experience.

"Were one of these—Perfected Beings—to take a student without such qualities into his field of work—he would be making the same mistake one does in building a machine or home, if he constructs it of imperfect material.

"That kind of material—naturally could not stand unusual strain, under sudden need, or prolonged service. Thus, it would not be the part of either wisdom, love, nor mercy to subject anyone to an experience for which he has—neither the training—nor is strong enough to bear. As the Ascended Masters are the Acme of Perfection—they naturally would not do anything except that which is just, loving and wise.

"The attitude of one who wishes to work in conscious co-operation with the Ascended Host should not be—'I wish I could go to them for instruction'—but rather—'I will so purify, discipline, and perfect myself, become such expression of Divine Love, wisdom, and power that I can assist in their work—then I will automatically be drawn unto them. I will love so constantly, so infinitely, so divinely, that the very intensity of my own—"Light"—will open the way for them to accept me.'

"My son, self-correction and control of the forces within the use of human consciousness—is not the work of a moment—nor a path of ease, lethargy, and self-gratification—for the senses riot within the average human being—and he rebels furiously against the restraint of his—lower nature—which is imperative—if he is to govern these forces properly within himself—especially in his feelings—so they may be used and act—only—under the conscious Dominion of his God-Mind.

"The saying that—'Many are called but few are chosen,'—is very true. All are constantly being called but—few—are awake enough—to realize—the Ecstatic Joy and Perfection within—the God-Self—and to hear Its Voice in the 'Light' forever and forever calling everyone back into the Father's House.

"Every individual on earth is free each moment to 'Arise and go unto the Father'—his God Self—if he will but turn his back upon the creation of the human senses and—hold his attention—on the—Only Source—in the Universe from which peace, happiness, abundance, and—Perfection—can come.

"There is a way for all to come into contact with the Ascended Masters, and that is to—think—upon them—call unto them—and they will answer every call with their own 'Presence' of Love—but the motive for the call must be—Love of the One Source—Love of the Light—Love of Perfection.

"If this be real, determined, and steadfast, the student—will—receive greater and greater—Light—for the 'Light' knows Its own and gives of Itself, unceasingly, unconditionally, every moment. Ask and ye shall receive—knock and it shall be opened unto you—seek and ye shall find—call unto the 'Light' and the—Ascended Masters will answer you—for they are the 'Light' of this world.

"Lotus served as a priestess in the temple of Mitla—for more than forty years with you and your son. By the combined efforts of you three, the various cities in the colonies were brought to a state of great perfection. You established industries and directed the agriculture, until prosperity abounded in the land.

"It was revealed to the Inca Ruler, when he was to finish his earthly pilgrimage and service in that civilization. It was then—he called the three of you home to him. Others were appointed to take your places and with blessings and love to your people, you bade them farewell.

"On your arrival home, the King was much surprised to find—none of you had aged during the long absence. Your youthful appearance was the result of training received in childhood, and still greater proof that his children had been divinely sent in answer to his prayer. Deep gratitude, to the One Mighty God for blessing him, his children, and the people, always filled his heart."

At this point, as Saint Germain described the Incan embodiments—living pictures began to appear in the atmosphere before me—all in their—original—color and activity. They lasted for nearly three hours, and. he revealed those ancient experiences as a—Living Reality in Peru and Mitla.

The Inca Ruler—called the fourteen from the Golden City together—in preparation for the—most important event—of his earthly pilgrimage. He knew the hour of passing was near, and the affairs of the empire had to be transferred into the control of the elder son—whom he was to appoint his successor at the banquet.

The palace—was famous for centuries, as the most magnificent building of the period—because the King had tremendous resources at his command throughout the entire reign. He lived close to his God Self at all times—and wealth untold flowed into his use. The interior of the palace was most ornate, the private rooms of the royal family being decorated in—pure gold set with jewels—and the symbol of the Sun—used wherever possible, as a constant reminder of the God Self Within.

The banquet hall was set with five tables of—carved jade—resting on white onyx pedestals, each seating twenty people, with the exception of the royal table at which were sixteen—these being the fourteen from the Golden City, the King, and—the Master Saint Germain—who was then known as "Son Uriel." The chairs at the King's table were made of gold, slightly canopied with gorgeous ostrich plumes in magnificent colors. In the Inca's chair, the plumes were a beautiful violet; in Saint Germain's an intense gold; the daughter's pink; the eldest son's violet; but of a lighter shade than the ruler's—and those in the chair of the younger son—white—representing the authority—of the priesthood. The plumes in the chairs of the rest of the fourteen from the Golden City were of—varying colors—beautiful beyond description, the color in each case—representing the office and service—that each occupant gave—to the empire.

Cloths of a very soft material, heavily embroidered with thread of remarkable brilliancy, covered the tops of the tables. The entire palace was lighted by—self-luminous, crystal globes—that Saint Germain gave to the Incan ruler, when his instruction first began.

The King wore a royal robe of golden, metallic-like fabric with a marvelous jeweled breastplate representing the—"Sun." Over this was his robe of office, made of rich, purple fabric trimmed with magnificent ostrich plumes around the entire edge, and deep collar. His crown was a band of diamonds, that held three violet plumes at the back. These three plumes in the Inner Life of the ruler symbolized the three activities of the Godhead—Father, Son and Holy Spirit—acting through man as Love, Wisdom, and Power. The two sons were clothed in garments similar to their father's, except for the long robe of state, each wearing the symbol of the—"Great Sun"—formed by a breastplate of jewels. The crown of the elder son was set with emeralds and the plumes at the back were violet like the king's, but of a lighter shade. The head-dress of the other son was set with pearls, and his plumes were white—another symbol of his office—as priest.

The king's daughter was robed in a golden fabric—fine as gossamer silk—with an over-drape of opalescent material, dazzling to behold—that changed color with every movement of the body. She wore a jeweled girdle of diamonds and emeralds with its panel reaching nearly to the floor. On her head was a close-fitting cap of woven material, and around the neck a chain—on which hung the symbol of the "Great Sun" set in diamonds, rubies, and emeralds. Her sandals were of gold—also jeweled.

Just as the King left his private chambers on the way to the banquet hall, a—Blazing Light—flashed through the rooms, and Saint Germain stood before us—looking like a God. The "Light" about him was almost blinding in its Brilliance and we were a few seconds becoming accustomed to it.

His beautiful golden hair hung to the shoulders, and was held in place by a band of—blue diamonds—around the forehead. His own Intense Radiance shone through the color of the hair—until it looked like sunlight. The piercing, sparkling violet of his eyes contrasted strongly against his skin—that revealed the soft pink color of youth and perfect health. His features were very regular—like those of the ancient Greeks.

He wore a robe of—marvelous—dazzling white fabric—entirely different from anything—in our modern world. It fitted the body slightly at the waist around which was clasped a—girdle of yellow diamonds and sapphires—with a panel reaching to his knees. On the third finger of his left hand was a ring set with a—gorgeous yellow diamond—and on the middle finger of his right a—sapphire almost as brilliant—both blazing tremendously because of his own great Radiation—as he had just come from the—Golden City.

The King was surprised and overjoyed at his appearance—and making the sign of the heart, the head, and the hand—bowed low before him and offered the Master his arm. They proceeded thus into the banquet hall.

Here, the tables had been laid with an entire service of gold, crystal, and jade. The children of the king soon entered and, when they beheld their beloved Master, were almost overcome with joy. However, they did not forget the dignity of the occasion and, making the Divine Sign he had taught them—bowed low before their father and Distinguished Guest.

The signal was given and all were seated. The King sat at the head of the table, the Master, Saint Germain, at his right and next to him his daughter. The elder son was placed at his left and the younger son next, then the rest from the Golden City.

At the close of the banquet, the Ruler arose and all gave complete attention. He stood silent a moment, and extending his hand to the beloved Saint Germain—introduced him to the guests. The Master bowed graciously, and the King told them how the Higher Spiritual Law had been taught to him and his children, and how the great blessings which had come to the land and its people, were the result of the Master's Great Love. He explained further that the banquet had been given for him to appoint his—successor to the throne.

He signaled to the elder son to rise and announced him—as their future ruler. Removing the Royal Robe—he placed it upon the son's shoulders and Saint Germain raising his hands above him in blessing, said:

"I bless you my son, in the Name and Power of the One Mighty God—in man and governing the Universe—whose Supreme Wisdom shall direct you—whose 'Light' shall Illumine you—whose Love shall bless and enfold you—the land—and its people."

Touching the thumb of his right hand to the forehead of the son, the Beloved Master raised his left hand and a Blinding Flash of "Light" enfolded them.

The king then appointed those who were to take the place of his daughter and two sons in the temple at Mitla. Saint Germain, the king, his children, and the rest of those from the Golden City, proceeded into the throne room, where the Master turned and again addressed them saying:

"Beloved ones of Light, your brother, the King, will soon pass to his well deserved rest and higher instruction. Until that time—I will remain with you. Your civilization will reach its apex under the rulership of this our beloved brother, and you will need much added wealth to accomplish all that is to be done. In the heart of the mountains not far distant, is great treasure of gold and precious stones.

"The younger son of your ruler has not so far recalled a faculty—he used formerly. I will quicken it into action again, that the requirement of your future activities be supplied." He stepped toward the younger son and touched his forehead with the thumb of his right hand. A tremor passed over the body and his—Inner Sight—became opened.

He saw—in the mountain fastness a certain location—which held such vast wealth—he knew they would need no other supply for whatever might be required to produce the things—they were to use in the outer activities. The son made obeisance to his Beloved Master and promised that—with his assistance—the plan for its use would be fulfilled. Three of the mines which he opened and operated were closed and sealed—when the reign of those from the Golden City was finished. They have remained closed—to this day.

Archaeologists—in various ways from time to time—are finding evidence and proof—of the tremendous height to which this civilization reached and the—splendor of its attainment. The fragments of the Incan activities—they have discovered so far—are of the civilization during its decline—but the day will come, when that which was expressed at its—apex—will be revealed to the blessing, enlightenment, and service of posterity.

The following day, messengers were sent to the principal points in the empire, announcing the ascension to the throne of the King's son. His reputation had preceded him from the City of Mitla, for his wisdom, nobility of character, and justice were known throughout the kingdom during the years he served there.

A few days later, the younger son directed the head mining engineer to prepare equipment, men, and supplies for going into the mountains and opening the mine he had been shown through the use of his—Inner Sight.

When they were ready to start, the son remained alone and held his attention fixed steadily on the God Self Within, knowing that he would be directed unerringly in finding the mine, and because of this—had no difficulty or delay in going directly to the location shown him in the vision. He put a large number of men to work, and in sixty days had opened the mine to the point where they made contact with the—richest gold vein that has ever been located in South America—before or since that time. The discovery and operation of that mine—has come down to the present day—in legend among the people. The younger son returned from his achievement amidst the warm welcome of the people, and received the blessings of his father, Saint Germain, his older brother and sister.

The location of the mine was at an altitude of eight thousand feet, and during the time the king's son was there he became highly sensitized—an activity that—always occurs—at high elevations. Upon his return to the palace, he felt clearly—the time had arrived—for the Inca Ruler to make the great change, and knew his passing was near.

The day arrived for the coronation of the King's son, when he was to legally and publicly assume the responsibility and duties of the realm. The royal family asked their Beloved Master and Friend to perform the act of crowning the new ruler—to which he graciously agreed.

Elaborate preparation for the important event had been completed, and the ceremony had progressed to the moment—when the crown—was to be placed upon the head of the new ruler. All noticed—that Saint Germain made no effort—to receive it.

Suddenly—there came a Blinding Flash of—"Light"—and before them stood a—Most Wonderful Being. She seemed to be a girl of only eighteen—but from her eyes and "Presence" shone forth a Dazzling Radiance, filled with the Love, Wisdom, and Power of a Goddess. The—Light—that filled the atmosphere around her, was crystal-white—sparkling within Itself—and scintillating—constantly.

Extending her dainty hands to the crown bearer—she lifted the crown—and with infinite grace—placed it upon the head of the King's son, and in a voice—that was the very soul of music said:

"Beloved of the Golden City—I crown you with Love, Light, and Wisdom of which—this crown—is the symbol. May your justice, honor, and nobility ever continue. By a—Divine Order—I shall reign with you invisible to all—but those of the Golden City—who are here."

The new ruler knelt to receive the crown and the—Wondrous Being—stooped and kissed his forehead. She then turned to the assembled guests, extended her hands, and blessed them. Immediately—a soft rose colored—Light—filled the entire place—It being the Outpouring of Her Love to them. She blessed the former king and turning to his daughter held her in a fond embrace. To the younger son she extended her hand—and he kneeling—kissed it with deep reverence.

The new king ascended the throne and bowed to his guests. Offering his arm to the Beautiful Being, he led the way to the banquet hall and here they celebrated the coronation by a feast. He gave the signal to be seated and then addressed them.

"My greatly beloved people," he said, "I know there is but One Mighty 'Presence'—God—in mankind and the Universe, governing all. It is my desire, as it ever has been, to so live that my mind and body are clear channels and perfect expressions of the—One Great Indwelling 'Presence.' May you my friends, my people, our land, and its activity be always blessed with God's greatest love, peace, health, and happiness. May this empire—which is God's domain—and of which we are but the custodians, continue in abundant prosperity. The Love of God in me shall always enfold you, and I ask God's Eternal—'Light'—to raise you into His Divine Perfection."

As the banquet progressed, the Former King grew very pale. The new ruler signaled his brother who stepped to his father's side, and assisted him to the private rooms of the royal family. The King lay down and remained motionless nearly four hours. His children, the Master Saint Germain, and the Beautiful Being remained at his side.

When the final moment of his earth span arrived, the Beautiful Being stepped forward to the head of the couch on which he lay, and addressed him, saying:

"Brother Inca—thou hast thought to leave thy form to the action of the four elements—but I say to thee—it shall be Raised—Transmuted—and Illumined—into that Eternal 'Temple of God' that expresses All Perfection. Thy great service has freed thee from the wheel of birth and death. Be thou—now—received by the Ascended Host of Light—with whom thou art forever—One."

Slowly—the body began to fade from sight—dissolving into a fine mist—and then completely disappeared. Saint Germain turned to those who stood by.

"My work here is finished," he said, and stepping forward, placed a ring—of most unusual design upon the third finger of the king's right hand. Its jewel was a—miniature self-luminous globe—of some kind of precipitated substance—that looked like pearl, and directly within the center was a—tiny blue Flame. It was a focus of "Light"—the same as the globes Saint Germain had given the king's father—with which the palace was lighted.

"Accept this," he continued, "from the—Master of the Golden City. It is his request—that you wear it upon your person—always." Bidding them farewell and bowing graciously, he disappeared from sight.

The Inca's three children had perfect physical bodies, due—to the instruction they had received in childhood—from the Master Saint Germain, when he came daily from the Golden City to prepare them for their life service to the people. All had most beautiful golden hair and violet blue eyes. The two sons were fully six feet three inches in height and the daughter about five feet seven. There was a great natural dignity of bearing—suggesting the Inner Dominion, which they had gained under his instruction. When the elder son ascended the throne, he was sixty-eight years old, yet looked not more than twenty-five. Even at the time they left the earth—none looked more than that age. The new king reigned forty-seven years, living to the age of one hundred fifteen. The daughter lived to be one hundred thirteen and the younger son one hundred eleven.

The Incan people of that period were all dark eyed and dark haired—with skins like the American Indian. Those, who incarnated as the mass of the Incan people, were not souls of previous advanced knowledge, as was the case in some of the former civilizations such as Egypt, Atlantis, and the Sahara Desert. For this reason—the Great Host of Ascended Masters—who direct the evolution of humanity on this earth, placed the Incan ruler, his children, and the rest of the fourteen from the Golden City in charge of the government and its people—to establish the pattern—upon which the later activities were to be molded. They designed a form of government and a plan of development which—if adhered to—would have enabled the entire civilization to reach a great height of outer accomplishment—and at the same time—receive tremendous Inner Illumination.

As the time drew near to select a ruler from among the Incas themselves, to succeed the king and his assistants, great care was taken to choose those whose—Inner Growth was most advanced. Fourteen were found to take the places of those from the Golden City. The Beautiful Being had made herself visible to the king—every day—for forty-seven years, giving advice, and assistance through Her Radiation that wisdom and strength might be the directing power of the people.

The successors to the king and the fourteen from the Golden City were called into the presence of the much loved and wise ruler, and-the Beautiful Being—who had been invisible—made herself visible to all. The "Light" about her grew very bright—and she addressed them saying:

"For over ninety years—the Great Ascended Masters of Light—have taught, enlightened, blessed, and prospered the people and this empire. The example is before you. If you follow it, all will continue to prosper and bless your land. If you do not keep the Love for the One Supreme God Self—first—in your hearts and acknowledge him—always—as the Ruler of the empire and its inhabitants, decay will set in, and the glorious perfection, enjoyed for over a century, will be forgotten. I commend you to the care of the Great Supreme 'Presence' in all. May he ever protect, direct, and enlighten you."

Here—a visible proof of the existence of the—Inner God-Self—of each human being was revealed—to those who were to guide the destiny of the empire—during the succeeding years. This same example—will again be given—to the present people of America.

Then—in the presence of the new ruler and his associates—the king and the fourteen from the Golden City—stepped out of their bodies—and revealed—the Divine Self of each—visible—to all assembled. In a few moments the physical bodies disappeared—dissolving in ambient air.

"Thus," explained Saint Germain, "is revealed to you the record of another life, the blessing and achievement which results from—loving acceptance—of the Supreme 'Presence' of the One God-Self Within. Let us now go back to the Royal Teton."

We returned to the entrance and passed forward to the audience chamber. There—on its walls—were the portraits done on gold—transferred from the ancient temple of Mitla. We went on to the record room, and saw the records carried by the Beautiful Glistening Beings. Other things too had been brought—which I have not permission—to reveal.

As these experiences ended, I realized at least partially, something of what Real Love is, for no one can possibly explain the—intense feeling of love and gratitude—one has for the—Ascended Masters—after being permitted the experiences I had passed through since—first meeting Saint Germain. It can never be put in words. There is only one overwhelming desire in Life—after such contact—and that is to "BE" what they are.

Then, one comes to realize what Jesus meant by the Father's House, and where the home of the Soul—really is. Once he has really—even for the fraction of a second—experienced the Ecstatic Bliss Radiating from an Ascended Being—there is nothing in human experience he would not endure or sacrifice—in order to reach that height of attainment—and work for in order to express such Dominion and Love also.

One—Really knows—such Perfection—is—for all of God's children and is as—Real—as Reality can be. Even the happiest life lived—by the average human being—is certainly the husks of existence, compared to the—Ascended State—of these Great Ones. The most beautiful and, so called perfect, creation of human beings with all their boasted power and accomplishment is coarse and crude, compared to the Freedom, Beauty, Glory and Perfection that is the—daily—continual—experience—of every one—who has raised the body—as Jesus did.

I was almost overwhelmed by a feeling of gratitude and love to Saint Germain, as it came time to return to my body. He realized how I felt and understood my position.

"My son," he said, "you cannot receive what has not been earned. You deserve this and much more—which will become evident—as we advance. Remember, however, what seems mysterious—only appears so—because it is unexplained. When understood, all unusual occurrences will be found—natural—and according to—Law. The following Truth shall remain engraved on your memory forever. It is this:

"Every one of God's children who will—acknowledge and accept—the 'Presence' of the—One Mighty God—anchored Within his heart and brain—and feel that Truth deeply—many times a day, realizing and knowing God fills his mind and body—so full of—'Light'—there is no room for anything else—he can be free. The One All-Powerful 'Presence' is the Mighty Harmonious Activity of one's Life and affairs, and if his attention be fixed firmly—with determination—on this Eternal Truth—no height of attainment is—too great—for him to reach.

"There is but—One Source and Principle of Life—to which we should give our undivided attention—that is the—God Self—Within—every—individual. To the Great Harmonious Self—the personal self should give—conscious recognition at all times—and keep in constant Inner Communion with It—no matter what the outer activity of the mind is.

"This One Great Self is the Life-Energy flowing through every human body each moment—by Which—all—are enabled to move about in the world of form. It is the Wisdom flowing through the mind—the Will directing all constructive activities—the Courage and Strength sustaining every one—the Feeling of Divine Love with Which—all force—can be qualified as it flows through the individual—and the Only Power—that can ever accomplish any good thing. It is the—All-Victorious, Conscious Dominion—over every condition of human activity, when released through the personal self—without resistance or interruption.

"This Mighty God Self is Within you, is the Supreme Ruler of all creation, and the only Dependable, Permanent and Eternal Source of Help in existence. Only through—Its—Love, Wisdom, and Power can anyone ever rise into the Ascended Mastery—for constant—conscious—communion—with It—is Freedom—and Dominion over all human creation. When I say human creation—I mean all that is discordant and less than Perfect."

We returned to my body, and as soon as I had reentered it, Saint Germain took my hands and poured a stream of his Divine Energy through me to sustain and give strength. I instantly felt revivified in both mind and body. I sat down, fixed my attention with deep intensity upon my own God "Presence," and offered up a prayer of gratitude for the tremendous blessings I had been privileged to receive. He bowed graciously and disappeared.

CHAPTER - VI

Buried Cities of the Amazon

A SHORT time later, I was working intently one evening, when I heard Saint Germain's voice distinctly.

"Be ready," he said, "tonight at nine o'clock, and I will come for you."

I was alert in an instant, hurried through my work, bathed, and was preparing for an early dinner.

"I will bring you the proper nourishment," he explained, so I waited and entered into the deepest meditation of which I could be aware, recognizing only—God's Perfect Manifestation.

Promptly at nine o'clock, he appeared in my room—wearing garments of Glistening Metallic-like Substance that looked, as if made of burnished steel—but felt like a combination of very soft silk and rubber—extremely light in weight. I touched the beautiful, wonderful fabric and was so fascinated that—I stepped forth from my physical body, and was unaware of it, until I turned and saw it lying in bed. Stepping forward to a large mirror in the door, I saw—my—garments were exactly like those of Saint Germain. I wondered at this, and did not understand—why they were different from the—ones—in which we had gone forth before. He saw that question in my mind and answered it.

"Try to realize, my son, that in the—Ascended Condition of Life—we are—always free—to use the Pure, Universal Substance for whatever purpose we choose, and give it any specific quality—we desire—for the requirement at hand.

"If we wish to use material that is—imperishable—we impose that quality upon the Pure, Universal Substance, and It—responds accordingly. If we wish a form to be manifest only a definite length of time, we give the Substance, of which it is composed—that quality or command—and the form manifests accordingly. In the present instance, we are going to pass—through water—and the Radiation from the material in your garment so surrounds your finer body—as to insulate you from the natural qualities and activities—of the water element.

"Try to think upon this Power, which is—within—you. Call into use the great sea of Universal Substance from which you may draw without limit. It obeys—without exception—the direction of thought, and records any quality imposed upon it, through the activity of the—feeling nature in mankind.

"Universal Substance is—obedient—to your conscious will at—all—times. It is constantly responding to humanity's thought and feeling—whether they realize it or not. There is no instant—at which human beings are not giving—This Substance—one quality or another, and it is only through the—knowledge that the individual has conscious control and manipulation of a limitless sea of It—that he begins to understand—the possibilities of his own Creative Powers, and the—responsibilities—resting upon him in the—use—of his thought and feeling.

"Mankind—through the centuries has qualified the Universal Substance with perishability and limitation—and the bodies it uses today are expressing—those characteristics. The entire human race has storms of hate, anger, revenge et cetera within its feelings—and the four elements—which have recorded those qualities—return them to man through the world of nature—as storms. The people of earth have cataclysms of thought and feeling—as resentment against each other, against injustice, against places and things—knowingly and unknowingly sending out the feeling of—revenge. The great sea of Universal Substance—upon which these qualities have been recorded—and imposed—expresses them back to their source—the individual—by means of the four elements—as cataclysms—in Nature.

"Such activities are but Nature's ways of purifying and shaking herself—free—from the contamination of—human—discordant thought and feeling, and returning—to her Pristine Condition—of God's Purity.

"Every moment, each individual is receiving into his—mind and body—the Pure and Perfect Life of God. Each moment, he is also giving quality of some kind to the Pure Universal Substance of God. This quality—he alone creates and generates—and he must receive it back into—his mind and body—for all things in the Universe move in circles, and thus, return unto their—source.

"The Ascended Masters—have learned the—'Law of the Circle'—'The Law of the One.' Hence, we impose upon the Pure Universal Substance—only—the quality we wish to use, for the special work in hand. If we desire a manifestation to express a certain length of time—we set the time—give the command—and the Substance of which that special manifestation is composed—responds accordingly.

"In the case of the records—at the Royal Teton—and certain retreats throughout the world—it is necessary for our work—that certain things be made imperishable, in order to be maintained during the centuries. We decree—that quality—into them, and they record exactly our decree, for—Nature never lies. She is a Truthful recorder of the qualities playing upon Her. She obeys us, and also obeys man, but there is a certain activity within Her—that mankind is either in ignorance of—or else stubbornly refuses—to acknowledge. For this ignorance and stubbornness—it pays—and pays—and pays—continually, until the individual personal self learns and does acknowledge—this—Fundamental Eternal Truth: It is—'The Law of the One'—'The Law of Love'—'The Law of Harmony'—'The Law of the Circle'—'The Law of Perfection.'

"When humanity really does learn that 'Fact' and obeys—Its Everlasting Decree—the discords of earth and the destructive activities of the four elements—will cease.

"There is a Self-generating and Self-purifying Force within Nature that rises, and throws off all that disagrees with the—'Law of the One.' This force or Energy is a Pushing Activity from within out, and is—the One Power—expanding. If discord is imposed upon Pure Universal Substance, the electronic energy becomes temporarily damned up within it. When such accumulated energy reaches a certain pressure—expansion takes place—shattering the discord and limitation. Thus, 'The Great Life of the One.'—'The Ever-Expanding Luminous Essence of Creation'—'God in Action'—overpowers whatever seeks to oppose It, and goes on Its appointed Way the—Supreme Ruler—of the Universe. The Ascended Masters of Light—know this—and are 'One' with that knowledge.

"Mankind may know it, and be at 'One' also—if they only will. It is within the capabilities and possibilities of every individual—for It is the Innate Eternal Principle—Within—Self-Conscious Life. All human beings are—Self-Conscious Life. This Principle plays no favorites, and—all—can express Its fulness—if they really so desire.

"Within the—Life—of every human being is the—Power—by which he can express—all—that the—Ascended Masters express—every moment—if he but chooses to do so. All Life contains—Will—but only—Self-Conscious Life—is free to determine—upon its own course of expression. Hence, the individual has—free choice—to express either in the human, limited body or the—Super-Human, Divine Body. He is the chooser of his own—field of expression. He is the Self-determining—Creator. He has willed and chosen to live as—Self-Conscious Life.

"When one individualizes—within the Absolute, All-Pervading Life he chooses of his own free will to become an—intensified individual focus—of Self-Conscious Intelligence. He is the conscious director of his future activities. Thus, having once made his choice—he is the—only one—who can fulfill that destiny—which is—not inflexible circumstance—but a definitely—designed—plan of Perfection. It is—a blue print—which he elects to express in the realm of form and action. So you see, my son, a human being may at any time determine to rise out of his human qualities or limitations—and if he will give—all—of his Life, his Energy, to that determination he will succeed. Those of us who have raised the body accomplished the—'Ascension'—by giving—

all—unto the God-Self Within—and hence, It expresses through us Its Perfect Qualities—'The Divine Plan of Life.' Come, let us go."

As we started on our journey, I was conscious of going south and east. We passed over Salt Lake City, New Orleans, the Gulf of Mexico, The Bahama Islands, and then came to a silver ribbon which I knew to be a river. This we followed to its mouth. As we proceeded the God-Voice Within me said:

"It is the Amazon."

"Now, be conscious," instructed Saint Germain, "that the God in you is always directing and—Master—of every situation."

Just at that moment, we began to descend, and in an instant touched the surface of the water. It seemed firm—as solid earth—under our feet, and I experienced a feeling of surprise at the contact. He explained further—that we could go under water quite as well as to remain on top—for the garments we wore—radiated a protective aura—for a considerable distance around our bodies—and contained the conditions we needed—which enabled us to explore the subterranean stratas of earth and things—under water.

"This," he continued, "is due to what the scientific world would call—an 'electrical force-field' around our bodies—but the electronic force with which these garments are charged—is of a higher, finer electricity than that known in your-physical world. Some day, even your men of science—will stumble upon it and realize—it has always existed in the atmosphere—but they have not known how—to direct and control it—for the service of mankind.

"It is much more easily directed—by the mind—than by physical apparatus of any kind, yet it can be drawn and controlled through mechanical means. That which the outer world knows as—electricity—is but a crude form of the—Great Spiritual Energy of Life. It exists throughout Creation. As man raises and keeps his consciousness in contact with his Inner God-Self, he will become aware of the gigantic possibilities in the use of this higher power and force. Its service to him is—Infinite—in the creative work that he can do in all phases of activity."

We then entered the water, passing through it with—no resistance—at all. I was slightly startled at the novelty of the experience but remembered instantly the admonition to be conscious only of the—God Within me—as the Master—of every condition. Presently, we came near the shore and passed over many crocodiles—who saw us—but were undisturbed by our presence. Proceeding inland, we came to what looked like the top of a monument.

"This is the top of a sixty foot obelisk," explained Saint Germain. "There is only about ten feet above ground. It marked the highest point in a city of importance that was buried during the last cataclysm—when Atlantis was submerged. The obelisk is made of Imperishable metal and covered with hieroglyphics of that period. Notice, they are—very clear and will remain so—because of the Indestructibility of the metal. The city was originally built ten miles from the edge of the river—but at the time it was submerged—the mouth of the river was widened many miles."

We raised above the earth, and passed forward, following the Amazon to a point—fifty-six degrees west longitude. There, we took observations, and then proceeded to a point—seventy degrees west. Saint Germain explained—here was the locality for further observation and research. The section he indicated—covered the Amazon between these two points, and also two of its principle tributaries, the Jurua and Madeira rivers.

"This civilization," said Saint Germain, "was built during the period—between twelve and fourteen thousand years ago. The portion of the country we are concerned with is that section reaching from where—the Madeira River empties into the Amazon—to a point west—where the Amazon touches Columbia and Peru.

"Thirteen thousand years ago, the Amazon—was held within great dykes of stone. The entire country around it lay at an altitude of at least five thousand feet, and instead of the tropical climate it has today, a semi-tropical temperature existed the year round.

"For a great distance in this locality, the country formed a table land or plateau. Near the mouth of the Amazon were wide beautiful falls. The city, in which the obelisk stood, was built between the falls and the sea coast—about ten miles south of the river. There were great reptiles and vicious animals to be found in the Orinoco River—to the north." We came to a place near the Madeira River, and Saint Germain continued:

"This is the site of an ancient city—the capital of the empire and most important place in the civilization of that period." Here, he raised his hand, and it became as clearly visible, as any physical city is today.

"Notice," he explained, "how it was built in a series of circles and the business streets go out from its center, like the spokes from the hub of a wheel. The outer circles were pleasure drives built every third mile. There were seven of these making the city forty-six miles in diameter including the central circle. Thus, the business activities did not interfere with the beauty and convenience of the drives.

"The inmost circle was four miles in diameter, and within it were placed the executive buildings of the whole empire. The streets were all beautifully paved, and constructed eighteen inches to two feet below the surrounding buildings and grounds. They were flooded every morning, and washed thoroughly clean before the activities of the day began.

"Observe, the unusual magnificence of the pleasure drives, and how gorgeously beautiful were the plants and flowers forming the banks on both sides. One very predominant feature of their architectural design was that on the top floor of almost all the buildings, especially residences, were built adjustable domes. These could be opened or closed at will—as they were constructed in four sections and arranged so as to serve—for either sleeping or entertaining purposes. The days were never uncomfortably warm, and at evening the wonderful cool air from the mountains came as regularly as day appeared."

We entered the capital, an enormous structure of great beauty. The interior was finished in cream colored marble veined in green, and the floor, made of a dark moss green stone resembling jade in its texture, had been laid—so perfectly—as to seem almost like one piece. There were large tables in the rotunda—of the same kind of green stone as the floor—but lighter in shade. These had heavy bronze pedestals placed about three feet from each end. Here, Saint Germain again held out his hand—and we were among living people—moving through the buildings and grounds.

I held my breath astonished—for I saw an entire race of golden haired people—with beautiful pink and white complexions. The men stood fully six feet two to six feet four inches in height and the women averaged about five feet ten. Their eyes were a most beautiful violet blue, very clear and brilliant, expressing great, calm Intelligence. We passed through a door at our right, and entered the throne-room of the emperor. It was evidently his audience day—for he was receiving foreign and local guests.

"This was the emperor, Casimir Poseidon," said Saint Germain, in explanation. "He was truly God Incarnate. Note the kindly nobility of his face and—yet the tremendous power within him. He—was and is—an Ascended Master—Blessed and greatly beloved. For many centuries in myth and fable his memory was kept alive and the perfection of his kingdom described in epic poems, but as time passes into eternity the memory of such great accomplishments fades, and is often forgotten by succeeding generations."

Casimir Poseidon was every inch a Magnificent Ruler. He was fully six feet four inches in height, well built and straight as an arrow. When he stood, he towered above those around him and—the very atmosphere seemed charged—with Mastery. His golden hair was heavy and hung full to the shoulders. The royal robe was made of a material that looked like violet colored silk velvet trimmed in gold and under it he wore a close fitting garment of soft golden fabric. His crown was a simple band of gold with—an immense diamond—in the center of the forehead.

"These people," said Saint Germain, "were in direct contact with all parts of the world through marvelous aerial navigation that had been brought forth for their use. All light, heat and power were taken directly—from the atmosphere. Atlantis—during this period—was in a wonderful state of progress—because she had been governed and—shown the way to Perfection by various Ascended Masters—appearing from time to time and—ruling for the spiritual uplift of the people.

"Again and again all the way down the ages, whenever a great civilization has arisen it has been founded—on Spiritual Principles in the beginning—and maintained obedience to those Laws of Life—during the time of its ascendency. However, the moment any government or the people themselves begin to drift into lax ways, so that injustice and the unclean use of Life become habits either of officials or the people—disintegration begins and continues—until they either return—to the Fundamental Laws of Balance and Purity—or are wiped out by their own discord, that—the Balance may be re-established—and a new start given.

"Casimir Poseidon was a direct descendant—of the Mighty Ascended Master Rulers of Atlantis. In fact, the civilization over which he ruled was—a child of the Atlantean culture and attainment. His capital city was famous throughout the world—for its magnificence and beauty.

"As the rural districts are shown, watch the method by which objects are transported—for the power these people used was generated in an instrument-like box—two feet square and three feet long—attached to the mechanism of the implement in use. The water supply from the streams was placed under control and its power also utilized. There was no need for police or military organization of any kind because of the method—by which the people were reminded of—'The Law'—and the wonderful sustaining power that was radiated—enabling them to give obedience unto It."

To the east in the park, stood a magnificent building. We approached it. Over the entrance were placed the words—"God's Living Temple To Man." We entered, and found it much larger within than seemed apparent from the outside. There must have been seating capacity for at least—ten thousand people.

In the center of this immense temple—stood a pedestal about two feet square and twenty high—made of a Self-luminous milk-white Substance—that gave off—a White Light—with a breath of pink in it. Upon it stood—a crystal globe—two feet in diameter made of some kind of—Substance—holding a soft Self-luminous White Light—within. It was very soft, and yet so—Intensely Luminous—that the entire building was brilliantly lighted.

"That sphere," remarked Saint Germain, "was made of a Precipitated Material enclosing an Intense Focus of 'Light.' It was drawn—and placed in the temple at that period, by one of the—Great Cosmic Masters—as a sustaining and Life-giving activity for the People. It continually sent forth not only the—'Light'—but an Energy and Power which stabilized their activities and the empire.

"The sphere of 'Light' was focused by the—Great Being—and the building erected around it afterward. It was—really—a Precipitated Focus and Concentrated Activity of the Supreme God 'Presence.' The Great Cosmic Master—who established It—appeared once a month beside the 'Light' and proclaimed 'The Law of God'—'The Law of Government'—and The Law of Man.' Thus, he decreed—the Divine Way of Life—and was the Focus of the Christ Activity—for the people of that Age."

Here, Saint Germain stretched forth his hand again, and living, talking pictures of this—Great Being—passed before us. It is absolutely impossible to describe in words the—Glory—of that "Presence." I can only say—he was truly the—Son of God—in Perfect Expression. In a moment, I heard the—Great Cosmic Master—proclaiming—"The Law"—to the people.

The Record and Majesty of his "Presence" and "Decree" are burned into my memory for eternity—so clearly do they remain in my consciousness. I give His Decree to you—just as it still stands before me.

"Beloved Children of the One Mighty God—knowest thou not the Life thou art using is from the 'One Supreme Presence'—Eternally Pure, Holy, and Perfect? If thou dost aught to mar the Beauty and Perfection of that—One Life—thou cuttest thyself off from the Gifts of Thy God. Thy Life is the—Sacred Jewel—of Thy God's Love—the 'Source' of the Secrets of the Universe.

"Thy God dost trust thee with—His Own Heart's 'Light.' Cherish It—Adore It—and let It ever expand unto greater—Light—and greater—Glory. Thy Life is the—Pearl of Great Price. Thou art the—Keeper of God's wealth. See thou use It for Him only and—know—thou hast received the 'Light of Life'—for whose use—thou shalt give an accounting.

"Life is a continuous Circle—the Principle upon which thy city is builded. If thou dost create—That—which is like unto Thy 'Source'—and knowest His Love and Peace within thee, if thou dost use Thy Powers of Creation to bless only—then as thou dost move around thy circle of existence—thou wilt know the Joy of Life—and unto It shall be added Greater Joy. If thou createst not like thy 'Source', thine evil shall return unto thee—with more of its kind.

"Thou alone dost choose thy destiny—and thou alone—answerest to Thy God—for the use thou dost make of 'Life'—Thy Being. The Great Law—no one can escape. Long, have I proclaimed this 'Law of Life.' The Law of 'Thyself—Thou are unto thyself, because thou canst always come unto Thy God—if thou desirest the Perfection of Life.

"I come not always as now—to hold thy straying feet upon the Pathway of Truth—nor to remind thee of—Thy Eternal 'Light'—set upon a mountain top for thy guidance. In a far distant day—I will speak within the Heart of man, and if thou dost Love Life—thou wilt call unto Me—abiding in many selves. Let this not confound thee, my children. If thou wouldst know Me—The Light'—thou wilt have to seek Me—find Me—and having found, abide within Me always.

"In that day, the 'Father—Mother—Son' will be 'One' in the Heart of man. The Son is forever the Door—the Way unto God. In thy mind and in thy heart is 'My Light'—ever reminding thee of 'My Presence'—for in the time to come, I will be present only in—That Light.'

"Then, will I Be Wisdom in thy Mind to govern the Love in thy heart—that thou mayest be filled with the Peace of The One Life—God. Thy body is but the instrument of thy Soul, and into thy Soul must stream—'My Light'—or thou wilt perish.

"My Light—in thy mind is 'The Way' into the Heart of All Light. Only by My Light in thee—canst thou expand—the Light in every cell of thy Being—into greater and greater Being. In thy throat is My Light—which is Thy Power to speak—My Words. Through these—I always illumine, protect, and perfect my children. Words that do not this three-fold mission—are not My Words—and can only bring misery—when spoken.

"Meditate upon My Light in thy mind—in thy heart, and thou shalt See within all things—know all things—and do all things. Then that which is not of Me can never confound thee.

"I speak these words now—and they shall be engraved upon the tablets of earth and the memory of its children. In the far off day of which I speak—one of God's children shall receive—these my words—and shall give them forth to bless the world.

"In that time, when thou hast fully received 'My Presence'—and art letting It always act in thy Life and thy world—thou wilt find the cells of the body—thou dost then occupy—becoming bright with 'My Light' and thou wilt realize thou canst continue on into that 'Eternal Body of Light'—the Seamless Robe of Christ. Then and then only, wilt thou be free from the wheel of re-birth. Having traveled thy long journey through human experience, and fulfilled the Law of Cause and Effect—thou shalt transcend all conditions governed by—Law—and shalt Thyself have become 'The Law'—All Love-'The One.'"

"Such is the Eternal Ascended Body of Christ," said Saint Germain turning to me, "in which one is able to wield the Scepter of Dominion—and be Free. My son, even now you can ascend into—'The Light of the One'—for—The Light—is in your mind—The Light—is in your heart, and if you will stand in It firmly, you can and will raise your physical body of limitation into your 'Pure Eternal Body of Light'—forever youthful and free, transcending time, place, and space.

"Your Glorious Self stands ever waiting for you. Come into—Its Light—and receive Eternal Peace and rest—in action. It—needs no preparation. It—has All-Power. Come fully into the embrace of your 'Light-Self' and that moment—even today—your present body can become Ascended."

As he finished speaking, the pictures ceased. We went a short distance further on, and stopped at a place where a large flat stone lay on the ground. As Saint Germain focused his power upon it—the stone raised from the earth and moved aside—disclosing an opening with steps leading downward. We descended about forty feet, and came to a sealed door. He passed his hand quickly over the door, unsealing it, and revealing certain hieroglyphics. "Center your attention on this writing," he instructed.

I did so, and saw the words—"God's Living Temple To Man,"—stand out clearly on the door before me. There—in front of me—stood the physical door—we had just seen a short while previously—in the living pictures.

The door opened, and we entered a room under one of the small domes built at each corner. In this, were a great number of metal boxes about two feet long, fourteen inches wide and six inches deep. Saint Germain opened one, and I saw they contained sheets of gold—on which the records of that civilization had been written with a stylus.

I realized—there must be rooms which had been sealed and preserved—under each of the four small domes, and that the large central dome had been built over the "Sphere of Light." We found a secret passage connecting the four small rooms, passed on to the second of these and saw the containers filled with—jewels belonging to the temple.

The third room contained golden and jeweled ornaments, the throne chair, and other chairs of gold. The throne chair was a striking example of the goldsmith's magnificent workmanship. The back formed into a shell making a canopy over the head of the ruler, and from its sides, hung golden drapes made of tiny golden links each forming a figure eight. These were looped back against the chair making a delicate and extremely graceful effect.

In the center of the room, was a table about fourteen feet long and four feet wide made of—real jade—resting upon a golden bronze pedestal. Near it—stood fourteen jade chairs—whose feet were tipped with gold, the seats curved and—the backs beautifully carved. On top of the back of each chair, as though standing guard—rested a beautiful phoenix made of gold—the eyes set with yellow diamonds. This design symbolized the immortality of the Soul, and the—Perfected Divine Being—each individual becomes, as he rises through the fire of suffering—from the ashes of his human creation.

The fourth room contained seven different types of power boxes—as I called them—that received and transmitted the force—drawn from the Universal, for lighting, heating, and propelling power. The records—showed these people were in contact with—all parts of the world through wonderful airships. Following this civilization came one known as the Pirua—and after that the Incas—both stretching over a period of thousands of years.

Shortly before the city, just described was buried, it reached the height of its glory and the Great Cosmic Master, who had drawn the Light by which it was developed and sustained—appeared for the last time to that empire. He came to warn of impending disaster, and would have saved its inhabitants—had they heeded him.

He foretold the cataclysm that swept the empire into oblivion before five years had passed and announced, it was his last appearance among them. Those—who wished to save themselves—were instructed to leave that part of the country—and were directed where to go with the warning—that the final activity would be sudden and complete.

As he finished the prophecy—his body faded rapidly from sight—and to the consternation of the people—the pedestal and the crystal globe holding the—Eternal Light—disappeared with him. For a time the populace were disturbed by the forecast of events affecting their empire—but after a year passed and nothing occurred, the memory of—His Presence—became dulled, and doubt began to creep in—as to the fulfillment of his decree.

The emperor—and those more advanced in spiritual growth left the kingdom—and came to a certain place in the western part of the United States—where they remained in safety until the change had taken place.

The great mass of the people who remained became more and more skeptical, and after two years one among them more aggressive than the rest attempted to set himself up as emperor. When the real emperor had left the kingdom—he sealed both the palace—and the temple—in which the "Light" had been maintained. The would-be-emperor attempted to force an entrance to the sealed temple and fell—lifeless—at its door.

Near the end of the fifth year at noon on the fateful day—the sun was darkened—and an awful terror filled the very atmosphere. At sundown, terrible quakes shook the earth and demolished the buildings into unbelievable chaos.

The land—which is now South America lost its equilibrium—and rolled to the east—submerging the entire eastern coast one hundred and sixty feet. It remained so for several years—and then gradually righted itself to within sixty feet of the original position—where it remains today.

That activity caused the widening of the Amazon. Previously the river was eighteen miles wide, deeper than it is today, and navigable from end to end. It flowed from what is now Lake Titicaca in Peru to the Atlantic Ocean. In a former time, there had been a canal built from the Pacific to Lake Titicaca, and this connecting with the Amazon formed an entire waterway between the two oceans.

The name of the continent at that time was Meru, it having been given the name of—a Great Cosmic Master—whose principle focus of activity was at Lake Titicaca. The meaning of the name Amazon, is—"boat destroyer"—which has come down the centuries from the cataclysmic period—referred to above.

The rolling of the entire continent of South America explains many conditions on its western coast—that geologists and men of science have been unable to explain—from the scientific data they have discovered—up to the present time.

Thus, do the great cataclysms of Nature draw the cosmic veil over civilizations of splendid achievement, and only fragments of these come to light as time passes into eternity. This Truth—may be doubted by the outer world—but the records, of that civilization—now reposing in the Royal Teton—will one day be its proof—reveal its existence, and the accomplishment—of that former age.

As I was shown these tremendous activities, I wondered why a civilization could be brought forth so wonderful, beautiful, and perfect in every way, and then go down—through the terrible destructive activities of a cataclysm. Saint Germain saw the question in my mind and volunteered the following explanation:

"You see," he said, "when a group of mankind is fortunate enough to come under the instruction and Radiation of—a Great Master of Light—such as this Great Cosmic Being is—they are given an opportunity of seeing—what the Plan of Life is for humanity, and the Perfection they are intended to bring forth and live in—by their own conscious effort. However, unfortunately, and it has been so many times down the centuries—the people will not try to understand—Life—but let themselves drop into a state of lethargy. They do not exert the necessary effort required to accomplish these things—by the power of God—within the individual. They begin to lean—on the One giving the Radiation. The sustaining power is only withdrawn, when the individual ceases to make conscious effort to understand—Life—and willingly work in harmonious co-operation with it.

"They rarely realize—most of their blessings are the result of the sustaining power—from the One giving the Radiation. If a certain group of souls have been taught the—Way of Mastery—and reminded lifetime after lifetime of their Divine Birthright—the hour arrives—when no more assistance is permitted. It is then—the Radiation of the Ascended Masters is withdrawn—and those souls are compelled to come face to face with the fact—the sustaining and accomplishing power was not due—to their own effort.

"These must understand—they can only receive that—for which an effort is made. In such activity, the experiences passed through—compel them to make the necessary self-conscious application—and when that is accomplished—expansion and God-Dominion begin to express.

"There is no failure for anyone—who continues to make self-conscious effort to express Dominion of the Divine over the human—because failure only comes—when self-conscious effort ceases. All experience—through which the individual passes—exists for one purpose only, and that is to make him—aware of his 'Source.' He—must learn—who he is, recognize himself as a Creator and—as such—Master of what he creates.

"Everywhere throughout the Universe—whenever the power to create is given to a Being—the responsibility of creating is always co-existent—with the power. All creation is by Self-conscious effort, and if the individual upon whom this—Great Gift of Life—has been bestowed refuses to take his responsibility—and do his duty, his experiences in Life will prod him with misery—until he does, for mankind never was created in a condition of limitation and it can have—no rest—until the Perfection—with which it was endowed in the beginning—is Fully expressed. Perfection—Dominion—Harmonious use—and Control of All Substance and Force is the 'Way of Life,'—the Original Divine Blue Print for humanity.

"God Within the individual—is—that Perfection and Dominion. It is that 'Presence' within the heart of everyone which is the—Source of Life—the Giver of every good and perfect thing. When the individual looks to and recognizes his—Source—as the Outpouring of All Good, he that moment automatically starts the flow of All Good things unto him and his world because—his attention—to his 'Source' is the—Golden Key—that opens every good thing unto him.

"The Life in every person is—God—and only by the Self-conscious effort to understand Life, and express the Fulness of good through himself—can the discord in the outer experience cease. Life—the Individual—and The Law—are 'One' and so it is—unto Eternity.

"Come," he continued, "we will go to a buried city near the Jurua River."

We traveled west, and soon came to a slight elevation. Saint Germain extended his hand, and again vivified—the Etheric Records of those people. The place we observed was—the second city of importance in the empire. The one from which we had just come was—the focus of spiritual power and activity, while the second, we were now to see, was the seat of commercial and governmental operations concerned with the physical welfare of the population. Here, was located the national treasury, mint, governmental, experimental, and inventive activities.

Not far distant from this city, rose the Mighty Andes, the source of the immense mineral wealth of the empire. I noticed one thing among these people that seemed most remarkable. All—were so completely at peace—and thoroughly contented. They expressed quiet and exquisite rhythm as they moved about. The pictures came to an end, and we proceeded to the only rocky spot visible.

Saint Germain touched one of the rocks. It moved aside, and we saw a flight of twenty metal steps leading down. These we descended and came to a metal door. We passed through, went down twenty steps more, and found ourselves before a massive sealed bronze door. He reached to the right, and unsealed a square opening—in which were metal stops like those of an organ. He pressed two of these, the great mass slowly opened, and we stood in an immense room—with everything just as it had been in that far off time. It had been used as a display room for inventions et cetera—to which the public had access. All the fixtures were made of metal—combined with what looked like opalescent glass.

"This," said Saint Germain, "was made by a fusing process combining certain metals with glass in such a way—as to make the metal—strong as steel and Imperishable. One man in the present age came very near the discovery of the same process—for he had all but one element, and that—would have made it imperishable."

The entire room was lined with the same peculiar metal and three massive doors led from it. Saint Germain went to a box of stops, pressed three of them, and all the doors opened at once. We entered the first one and found a passage long and narrow, more like a vault than a room. It was lined with containers—filled with discs of gold about the size of a silver dollar, stamped with the head of the emperor and an inscription that read—"God's Blessing to Man."

Entering the second door, we found similar containers filled with—uncut jewels of all kinds. In the third room, the containers were flat, and held—thin sheets of gold—on which were written—the formulas and secret processes—used in that period

"Among these," said Saint Germain, "are many formulas and processes—which were not used in that former time. They will be given into the use of the present age."

He went back to the box of stops and pressed another. A fourth door opened—which I had not noticed before. This led into an arched tunnel or passage-way—connecting the treasury with the mint. It must have been at least a quarter of a mile long—and at the far end we entered—an enormous room.

It was the main part of the mint, and was filled with a maze of machinery—of most wonderful construction. Among many things I saw were machines used for stamping the gold and cutting and polishing the jewels. They simply fascinated one—so perfect was their operation. Here, Saint Germain showed me a specimen of malleable glass, clear as crystal.

In this room were great quantities of native gold nuggets—gold-dust—and gold ingots—weighing eight and ten pounds each. I was speechless—at such an amazing quantity of wealth in one place—and Saint Germain knowing how I felt, remarked:

"It is utterly impossible—for such quantities of wealth as you see before you—to be released unto the mass of mankind—because the selfishness within the commercial world at the present time—makes it the height of folly—to let humanity—waste more of Nature's gifts.

"God and Nature bestow their wealth lavishly upon the earth—for the use and blessing of the Souls who incarnate here but—the selfishness and lust for power—within the feelings of mankind—make them forget the 'Higher Way of Life,' and cause man's inhumanity to man.

"The few—who rise to control of the mass should have the Intelligence to know that—what helps the mass—helps the individual most—but if they refuse to recognize this—'Law'—self-destruction follows—brought about—by their own selfishness. Selfishness and the feeling of power to control others—blind the reason—and dull the perception—of the outer mind to its own dangers—and such individuals—ride headlong to ruin in every case—ruin spiritually—mentally—morally and physically—extending many times—into the third and fourth embodiment following.

"Only when mankind rises out of the mire of its own selfishness and lust—in all its forms—can human beings be entrusted—with all that God and Nature hold ready—for Right Use; but any individual, as he cleanses himself of his own selfishness and lust—may have the fullest use of all these riches, when he will use them harmoniously—and for the blessing of others. Individuals—can—make themselves ready to be custodians of these gifts—for in the age that is already ushered in—only those will have unlimited use of wealth—who have made themselves worthy—to be Trusted Keepers and Dispensers of this treasure. God and Nature provide these Gifts for man to use rightly and Right use alone—is the condition on which they may be received." Saint Germain crossed his hands upon his chest and continued:

"Mighty God—enter so firmly into the hearts of Thy children—that they want—Only Thee, then none shall want—for any of Thy Great Gifts."

He sealed everything as we had found it, and we returned to my body—which I re-entered quickly.

He again gave me the crystal cup filled with Living Substance, and said:

"My beloved son, you will be a very valuable helper and may God always bless you." With that blessing, he bowed and was gone.

CHAPTER - VII

The Secret Valley

ONE morning sometime later, I received a strange letter by post—asking me to come to a certain address—in Tucson, Arizona. It conveyed the idea—that the information to be given was of such a nature—as could only be explained in person. I considered the extraordinary way in which the request had reached me, and yet felt an Inner Desire to respond to the call.

In a few days, I went to the address given, rang the bell, and in a moment the door was opened by a tall slender gentleman about forty years of age, with iron gray hair and gray eyes, who stood perhaps six feet one inch in height.

I introduced myself, and he greeted me with a cordial, sincere hand shake which revealed unmistakably—his was an absolutely true and dependable nature. His eyes were steady and fearless, and he gave one the impression—that he possessed great reserve energy.

I felt an unusual Inner harmony about him, and knew it could only mean the starting of a deep and wonderful friendship. He too seemed aware of an Inner something—that made each of us feel attracted to the other. He asked me to come in, and be seated.

"You are here," he began, "at my request, and I am deeply grateful, strange as it must have seemed to you. Your address was given me by one of whom I shall speak later. In explanation, I have this to say—that I have made some very remarkable discoveries which I must ask you to accept on faith—until I can take you with me, and prove their Truth and Reality to you.

"I was advised to get directly in touch with you personally—as the only one to whom this should be revealed—and with which I am concerned. For a starting point, I shall have to begin with things that occurred twenty years ago.

"At that time, I had a beautiful wife. Now, I know she had great Inner growth of which, however, I was not aware. A son was born—whom we both idolized. For five years, our happiness was complete. Suddenly, without any warning or apparent reason—the child disappeared.

"For many weeks, we searched and searched, and did everything humanly possible to find him, but to no avail. Finally, we gave up all hope. His mother never recovered from the shock and five months later—passed on.

"She had made a strange request during the last few days of her life—that her body be held in the vault for seven days—after her passing and then cremated. It seemed rather peculiar to me—for at no time had we ever discussed anything—in regard to this subject. However, I complied with her wishes. Imagine my surprise five days after her funeral, when I received a call from the man in charge of the cemetery saying—he had found the vault open that morning—and the body gone. No clue to anything concerning the whole strange occurrence was ever discovered.

"Sixteen years later, I awakened one morning—to find a letter—upon the floor of my room—addressed to me but with no postmark. I picked it up, opened it, and read the contents—which left me mystified and incredulous. It read:

"'Your wife and son are living, well, and strong. Soon you will see them. Have patience until that time. Rejoice to know there is no death. At the appointed time—directions will reach you in this manner—which you are to follow—implicitly. All depends upon your absolute silence. You shall see, and receive full explanation of all that has seemed so mysterious. Then—you will understand why Truth is far stranger and more wonderful than fiction—for even the most extraordinary fiction—is but the record of a Truth—that is somewhere in the universe.

"'Signed,

"'A Friend'

p. 200

"My Friend, you can imagine my astonishment. At first—I did not believe a word of it. The third evening after this—I was sitting in front of my grate fire, when I heard my beloved wife's voice as clear and distinct—as if she were in the room beside me, saying:

"'Robert, My Beloved—I am alive and well, and our son is with me. We will be so happy, when you are with us again. Do not distrust the message. It is all true. You will be brought to us—if you do not allow doubt to shut the door. I speak to you through the Sound Ray which you will one day learn to use.' I could stand the tension no longer—and said:

"Show yourself to me, and I will believe." Instantly, the voice replied:

"'Wait a moment.' In about three minutes, a Brilliant Ray of Golden Light came into the room—forming a tunnel, at the other end of which, stood my beautiful wife. It was she—unmistakably.

"'Beloved,' she said, 'seeming miracles have taken place in the midst of your Life for years but because your attention has not been called in the right direction, we had to wait until this time. Trust the message that will come to you. Then—you will come to us—and I assure you a new world will open. To our great love there is no barrier.'

"Instantly—the Light Ray vanished and with It the voice. My joy knew no bounds. I could no longer doubt. I felt a relaxation, peace, and rest I had not known for years. Then—came weeks of waiting which I now know was a preparation going on—within me. At last the message, I longed for so much, came and with it a diagram and directions to be followed.

"I saw this would lead me into the high mountains southeast of Tucson, Arizona. I made preparation to go at once, saying to my friends I was going to do a little prospecting. I took a horse and pack animal, finding very little discomfort and no difficulty in following the directions given. If I could have gone as the crow flies, I would easily have covered the distance in two days.

"Just before sundown of the third day, I came to a blind canyon and would have passed it unnoticed, if it had not been for the diagram. I had just made camp, when it became dark. I rolled up in my blankets and soon dropped off to sleep, dreaming most vividly—of waking in the morning and seeing a young man—standing near by—looking at me.

"When I did awaken, to my astonishment—there stood the young man in Real Life—looking at me intently. He greeted me with a beautiful smile—saying:

"'My Friend, you are expected to follow me.' I noticed, he had my things in readiness and turning without further discussion, led the way toward the head of the canyon. After about an hour, we came to a stop because of a cliff that seemed to close the way before us.

"He turned, placed his hands upon the rock, and pressed against it. A section of the wall—perhaps ten by twelve feet—moved in to a depth of about one foot—and then slid to one side. We entered a tunnel that centuries ago—must have been the bed of an underground water-course. My companion closed the entrance behind us and, as we turned to go forward, a Soft Radiance spread everywhere—so we could see quite clearly. I was astonished at all I saw but I remembered the admonition I had received in my instruction—'to be silent.'

"We continued in the tunnel for more than an hour, and finally came to a massive metal door. This opened slowly at my companion's touch. He stood aside, and waited for me to pass through. I stepped out into the bright sunlight, almost breathless with delight at the beauty of the scene before me. Ahead of us, lay a valley of surpassing loveliness—about a hundred acres in extent.

"'My Friend,' said the young man, 'you have returned home after a long absence—all of which you shall soon understand.' He then led the way to a beautiful building, near the foot of a sheer cliff at the upper end of the valley. As we came nearer, I could see many kinds of fruit and vegetables growing in abundance, among them oranges, dates, English walnuts, and pecans. A beautiful waterfall poured over the cliff—making a limpid pool at its base. The building was a massive one, and looked as though it had stood there for centuries.

"We had almost reached it, when a beautiful woman in white appeared at the entrance. We came nearer—and my beloved wife—stood before us—more beautiful than ever. In another instant, I held her in my arms, and after all the agony I had been through in those years—it was almost more than I could stand. She turned, putting her arm, around the young man who had brought me, and said:

"'Robert, this is our son.'

"'Son!' was all I could say, so nearly was I overcome by my emotions.

"He stepped forward, put his arms around both of us, and we three—stood there for a moment in deepest love and gratitude—happy once more. I suddenly realized it was sixteen years since he had disappeared, and by now he must be twenty-one. He answered my thought, by saying:

"'Yes Father, I am twenty-one. Tomorrow is my birthday.'

"'How can you read my thought so readily?'

"'O, that is a very ordinary and easy thing for us. It is all quite natural, when you understand how to do it and really—quite simple,' he replied.

"'Come,' he continued, 'you must be hungry. Let us have something to eat.' With their arms around me, we entered the ancient building. The interior was finished in pink marble and white onyx. I was shown to a beautiful room where the morning sun flooded everything with its glorious radiance. I refreshed myself, and found a suit of white flannel—had been provided for me. I tried it on, and it fitted perfectly. This surprised me but again I remembered the admonition 'to be silent.' I went downstairs, and was presented to—a striking looking gentleman—about my own height with large, dark, piercing eyes.

"'Father,' said my son, 'this is our Beloved Master, Eriel. He is the one—who saved the lives of both Mother and me—and has trained us all these years—until you could be prepared to join us here. It was he—who sent you the message and directions to come—because the time had arrived for your definite training to begin.'

"We entered the dining-room which was magnificent, and I could not refrain from expressing my admiration. It had been placed at the south-east corner of the building on the main floor and was flooded with sunshine morning and afternoon. The walls were made of heavily carved walnut and the beamed ceiling, inlaid between the beams with motifs in hexagonal design. A solid piece of walnut at least two inches thick resting on an ornately carved pedestal, served as a table and looked as if it were thousands of years old. We took our places around it, and presently a slender youth entered. My son introduced him by saying:

"'This is our Brother, Fun Wey, whom Our Master brought from China, when he was an infant at a time—his Life was about to be taken. He is from a very ancient Chinese family, and is able to do many wonderful things. He has always wished to serve us, and we are privileged and happy to call him—Brother. He is one of the most joyous natures I have ever known.'

"Among the things for breakfast were luscious strawberries with delicious date and nut cakes. We went into the large living-room and the Master Eriel said to me:

"'At the time your beloved wife—who is your Twin Ray—would have passed on, I saw an opportunity to give certain assistance—which would enable her to reach the Ascended State—and thus have much greater freedom and wider capacity for service. It was my great privilege and joy to give that assistance.

"'I opened the casket—restored her to conscious action—and enabled her to raise the body. It had already reached a point of high attenuation—because her desire for the "Light" was very great. It was her intense adoration to and longing for the "Light" that made possible her Ascension. I explained this to her the day you thought she had passed on.

"'All three of you were children of mine in an embodiment—of long ago. A great love was generated then—which has lasted through the centuries. Her deep love made possible—the assistance and raising—that has been accomplished at this time.

"'Your son—who was stolen with the intention of being held for ransom—was brought to this canyon. The two concerned with his kidnapping began to quarrel, and one—planned to take the child's Life.

"'I appeared before them—and took him. They were paralyzed by their own fear—and neither ever recovered. Both passed on a few weeks later. If one deliberately takes the life of another human being—or determines mentally to take it—he has set a cause into motion that will surely take his own.

"'A feeling or desire—for the death of another person—will do the same thing—for it goes forth to the person, and then begins its return journey to the one who sent it out. Many times individuals allow resentment against injustice to flash forth, with an intense feeling to rid the world of a certain individual. This is a—subtle form—of the thought of death—and to the one who sends it out—it must return.

"'Many, many people bring about their own dissolution—by this very subtle activity of the human self—for no one ever escapes this "Immutable Law." There are many phases of Its reaction—and it is because humanity indulges—in such thoughts and feelings—that the race as a whole—has been experiencing the dissolution of body after body.

"'The number of mankind—that pass out through physical violence—is infinitesimal—compared to the deaths brought about—by these subtle activities—of thought, feeling, and the spoken word. The human race has been killing itself off—for thousands of years in this subtle way—because it will not learn "The Law of Life" and obey It.

"'"There is only One Law of Life, and that is "Love." The Self-Conscious, thinking individual who will not or does not—obey that—Eternal Beneficent Decree—cannot and will not retain the physical body—because all that is not Love—dissolves form and it matters not—whether it be thought, word, feeling or deed—intentional or unintentional—the 'Law' acts—regardless. Thoughts, feelings, words, and deeds are each but so much force acting—and eternally move in an orbit of their own.

"'"If man knew—he never ceases creating even for an instant—he would realize, through the "Presence" of God within himself—he could purify his miscreations—and thus be free from his own limitations.

"'"He spins a cocoon of human discord around himself—and goes to sleep within it forgetting—at least for a time, that if he can build it, he can also—break through. By using the Wings of his Soul—Adoration and Determination—he can break through his self-created darkness. Then, he lives once more at the—Center of his Being—in the "Light" and Freedom of his "God-Self."

"'"However, in the activity of you and your beloved family, or shall I say my beloved family, the cloud that has seemed to hold so much of sorrow is now turned inside out and reveals its glorious golden lining. You have now come within the—Radiant Splendor of the "Light"—from which you will never again recede.

"'"In most cases, if human beings knew the wonderful things that are sometimes planned for them, they would unknowingly prevent the approach of this greater good. You have been invited here, not only to join your loved ones, but to receive—definite instruction—concerning the existence, use, and direction of the Mighty God-Power—latent within you. When you understand how to release and control It, anything will be possible for you.

"'"Your loved ones used the Light and Sound Rays in communicating with you. This knowledge with its power will be explained, and you too shall be enabled to operate them—consciously and at will. You feel deeply, and when that characteristic is consciously governed, there will come an Awareness of the Mighty God-Power—that stands ready to be released—at any instant.

"'"You are to remain here for six weeks of training. and then return to the outer world—to use—the understanding you have received. Come again, at any time for you are now one of us.'

"I can never put in words—what those six weeks meant to me. To become aware of my own ability to use the instruction and application of such wisdom astonished me. Soon, I began to gain a confidence in myself—that made everything much easier. What seems so mysterious and unusual to the human—I found natural and normal—to this Stupendous 'Inner-Presence.'

"I had to realize that I was—Truly—the Son of God. As a Son of the—Source of all Good—the Limitless Wisdom-Energy obeyed my conscious direction, and when I directed it—as does a Master—produced results instantly.

As I gained confidence in my own ability to use the 'Great Law,' the fulfillment naturally became more and more rapid. I marvel yet—at the Ever-pouring Fountain of Love and Wisdom that streamed forth from this—Great Master. We love him with a deep devotion—greater than any love that could ever exist between parent and child—for the Love Tie formed by the giving of Spiritual Understanding is Eternal, and far deeper than any love generated through human experience—no matter how beautiful and strong it may be. He often said to us:

"'If you will make yourselves—an Eternal Fountain of Divine Love—pouring it forth into every place your thought goes, you will become such a Magnet for All Good—that you will have to call for help to dispense it. Peace and Calmness of Soul release a power—which compels obedience—of the outer mind. This must be—claimed—with authority. Our home here in this Secret Valley has been used for over four thousand years.'

"One day, after giving a remarkable discourse on 'God's Ownership,' he looked at me very intently, and suggested we take a walk. He led the way to the opposite side of the valley from which we had entered. Near the south wall, and running parallel with it from east to west, was a ridge beginning at the ground, rising to about seven feet in height, extending about two thousand feet in length, and then descending to the ground again. As we came closer, I saw it was a vein of white quartz. The Master Eriel stepped to where the vein came to the ground and kicked a piece loose with his foot. I saw it was—immensely rich—in gold. My human love for gold attempted to surge forth but the 'Inner-Presence' instantly checked it, and with a smile the Master remarked:

"'That is well done. Now, I have work to do in Europe and must leave you for the present.' He smiled, and was gone instantly. It was the first time—he had shown the Full Dominion he possessed, and the things—he was able to do in this manner. Immediately—my son became visible—in exactly the same spot—where Eriel had been standing the instant before and laughed heartily at my surprise.

"'Mother and I,' he said, 'can take our bodies with us—wherever we choose in the same way. Do not be surprised. It is a—Natural Law—and—only seems strange and unusual—because you are not using it—as yet. It really is no more extraordinary—than the telephone would have been—to the people of the Middle Ages. If they had known the "Law" of its construction, they could have used it then—just as well as we of this century.'

"Since that visit to my family in the Secret Valley, I have been there seven times. The last time, I returned to the outer world—the Master gave me your address—which accounts for my asking you to come here. He extends the invitation for you—to return with me."

My host suddenly realized he had been talking several hours, and begged indulgence for taxing my patience. I told him the experiences were so fascinating, and I had been so intensely interested that time was non-existent, so far as I was concerned. I accepted and was deeply grateful—for the Master Eriel's invitation to visit them, and said so frankly. A moment later, a tall young man came into the room.

"Let me present our Brother, Fun Wey," said my host, introducing him, and in the most perfect English, he replied:

"My Brother—with the Heart of Light—has journeyed far. My heart leaps in ecstasy and joy. My soul feels your Serenity and Radiance." Addressing my host directly, he continued.

"Knowing you were busy, I am here to serve you."

"It will give us great pleasure to have you break bread with us," said my friend turning to me, and together we passed into the dining room. Our dinner was delicious, and when finished my host again resumed his conversation—relating many of his personal experiences with Eriel. They were remarkable indeed—that is speaking from the human side of our consciousness only—but from the standpoint of our—Divinity—all was and is—Supremely Natural.

Suddenly, a Ray of Light—or rather a Tube of Light—came into the room, and from the conversation I knew it was my host's Twin Ray speaking. In a moment, the Ray was directed to me, and he said:

"Beloved, allow me to present the Brother—whom our Master Eriel has requested I meet."

I saw his Twin Ray, and heard her as clearly—as if she stood in the room beside us. This way of communicating is a wonderfully happy experience, and—it is possible—to so condense "Light" as to form a Tube in which Sound and Vision can be conveyed. It was as Real—as a search-light.

My host insisted that I make his home mine—until the day of our departure into the mountains. We started before daylight the seventh day after our meeting, and it was one of the most memorable experiences of my Life up to that time. All he had told me proved to be true—in the minutest detail.

Our arrival at the Secret Valley was a most joyous event, and our happiness was very great. I met my host's Twin Ray and their son, and was then shown over the ancient building—where so many students had received the True Understanding of the Laws of Being—and attained their Eternal Freedom.

It was a marvelous sensation—to stand where the Great God-Power had been focused for so many centuries, and—the Ascended Masters had made a retreat—for some of their work. I sat contemplating the blessings the students had received—who were privileged to come there, when the Master Eriel addressed me.

"My Son," he began, "you are nearing wonderful liberation. Hold close to the continuous acceptance of your own indwelling 'Master-Presence,' and you will have just cause for great rejoicing." He extended his right hand, and—the veil between the visible and invisible—was drawn aside.

"I want you to see," he continued, "as we who have Ascended—The Sublime and Majestic Activity of Our World. Here, we continually bear witness, as Sons of God, because there is no longer doubt, fear, or imperfection within us." I shall always remember the joy and privilege that was mine during the days I spent with those wonderful people.

"Every day," said Eriel, "you shall witness the use of the—Light and Sound Rays—that annihilate time and space, and which mankind is destined to use in the near future—as naturally as they now use the telephone. This is one of the most Stupendous Activities the individual may learn how to direct. A Light Ray can be drawn and controlled—so it may be used as a pencil—to write upon metal—or in the sky, and the writing—remain visible—as long as the one directing—desires.

"When the student is strong enough—to stand against the opinions of the world of ignorance—then he or she is ready—to bear witness to the—Marvels of the Individual Activities of God—manifested by the Ascended Masters.

"Until he can do this—the power in suggestion and the radiation of doubt from others will disturb him intermittently—to such an extent—that he many times gives up the quest for Truth. Interruption to the steady flow of instruction—is—discord. Discord is the wedge—and subtle way—by which the sinister force on this earth—enters the outer activity of a student—who has determined to face—'The Light.'

"Such activity is very subtle—because it is a feeling, and creeps in upon one before he is—really aware—of its existence. It is persistent beyond belief—and the growth is so insidious—that one does not realize what has been done—until the momentum is already under way.

"This feeling begins—as a slight doubt. A doubt need only be—felt—two or three times, until it becomes—distrust. Distrust—whirls a time or two in the emotional body—and becomes suspicion—and suspicion is self-destruction.

"Remember this my son, as you return again to the outer world, and you will find it a safeguard—that will carry you through every experience in Life—keeping you untouched by discord. If one sends out suspicion, he—will—be suspected, for every one has in his world just exactly—that—which he puts into it, and this 'Eternal Irrevocable Decree' exists throughout the Universe. All impulses of consciousness—travel back to the central point—that sent them out—not even an atom escapes.

"The Real student of 'Light' faces 'The Light'—sends it before him—sees its Enfolding Radiance—everywhere he moves, and adores 'It'—constantly. From the doubts, fears, suspicion, and ignorance of the human mind, he turns away, and knows—only 'The Light.' This is His Source—His True-Self."

With these parting words, Eriel bade me farewell, and I returned to the daily routine of my outer life.

CHAPTER - VIII

God's Omnipresent Power

THE following day, I received a communication through which I became engaged in a business activity that required all my time and attention. The mere anticipation of it gave me great joy, and I entered in with much enthusiasm. There came a refreshing, quickening sense, a thing I had never before known in my business experience.

In the course of its progress, I came into close personal contact with a man of very dominating character. His entire attitude in business was to gain his desire by force—if intrigue failed or he was opposed in any way.

He believed only in the power of his own intellect and human will, and had neither knowledge of nor faith in—anything else. At no time, did he hesitate to crush or ruin persons or things that stood in the way of his success, and used all means to gain his own selfish ends.

I had met him some three years before the following experience took place—and at that time had felt almost helpless in his presence—so overpowering was the feeling of domination he continually sent out. Yet, I knew in spite of my own reaction to him that his control over others was—only force—focused into the outer activity. I was somewhat disturbed, as I realized I would have to associate with him. Immediately, I sought a way to deal with him by application of the God-Law, when the "Inner Voice" said to me clearly:

"Why not let the 'Mighty God Within'—take full charge and handle this condition? That 'Inner-Power' knows no domination, and is—Always Invincible."

I was immensely grateful, and completely released everything into "Its" management. I met this man with two others, and agreed to go with them to inspect a mining property in a distant state. I felt it to be a very valuable one. The owner was an elderly lady whose good husband had passed on by an accident in the mine some months before.

He had left things in a precarious condition, and our dominating friend had determined to buy the mine at his own price—not an honest one. After a long trip by auto, we reached our destination about two o'clock the second day. We met the owner whom I realized was a blessed soul—true and honorable.

Then and there—I took the determined stand that she should have a square deal, and receive full value for the property. She invited us to a lovely luncheon, and we proceeded to examine the mine. We went through the workings, tunnels, drifts, shafts and stopings. The more I watched, the more certain I became something was wrong. The very atmosphere seemed to breathe it to me.

I was certain—a rich strike had been made—which had not been reported to the owner. I somehow knew the buyer had secretly placed one of the workmen on duty to watch for such an activity and that during the weeks of watching, he had gained the confidence of the superintendent. I realized at heart he was a good man but—not awakened spiritually speaking.

As we stood talking to him, my God-Self disclosed fully what had occurred. A short time previously, as these two were on their inspection of the work, they had come to a spot where the shots had broken into the face of a tunnel leading directly into the heart of the mountain. The blast had broken into—a very rich vein of gold bearing quartz. The superintendent was about to rush out, and report it to the owner, when the spying workman remarked:

"Wait! I know the man who is going to buy this mine. If you want to continue your present position, don't mention that strike. I'll see to it you not only stay here, as superintendent, but there'll be five thousand in it for you. The old lady'll get enough to keep her anyway," and the superintendent fearing the loss of his position had agreed.

In our examination of the mine, we came to the end of the main tunnel, and I felt strongly this was the place, the rich strike had been made. It had been cleverly covered up and disguised as a loose formation where it was dangerous to work. Such was the report they had made to the woman who owned the mine. As I stood at this place talking with the others, my Inner Sight was opened, and I saw all that had taken place, the rich strike, the covering of it, the offer to the superintendent, and his acceptance. I was grateful to have my feeling verified—but knew I must wait. We returned to the owner's residence, and negotiations began. The buyer opened the subject by saying:

"Mrs. Atherton, what do you expect for this property?"

"I am holding it at two hundred fifty thousand dollars," she replied courteously and gently.

"Absurd!" he shouted, "preposterous, ridiculous. It is not worth half that amount." He carried on in this vein for some few moments, blustering as was his habit. It had worked many times before, and he was still following the old line of procedure. He argued and stormed and ended by saying:

"Mrs. Atherton, you are in a position—where you must sell, I will be generous and give you—a hundred and fifty thousand."

"I will consider it," she replied, so cowed by his attitude of domination and bluster—that she began to accept his ideas and give in to his arrogant impudence. He saw her waver and immediately, began to high pressure the whole situation.

"I cannot wait," he went on, "my time is valuable. You must decide at once or the deal is off."

He drew the papers from his pocket and placed them on the table. Mrs. Atherton looked about helplessly, and I shook my head—no—to her but she did not see me. The contract lay open, and she stepped across the room taking a chair at the table—preparing to sign. I knew, if she were to be protected, I must act at once, and going to where she sat, I addressed our dominating friend.

"Just a moment, my good man," I said, "you will pay this dear lady what her mine is worth—or you are not going to get it." He turned his wrath upon me—with several very pungent invectives and attempted the same tactics—as usual.

"I'd like to know who is going to prevent me having the mine at—my price?" he retorted. I felt a surge of the—Mighty God-Power Within—come forth like an avalanche, keeping me unaffected by his tirade of vindictiveness, and I replied:

"God will prevent you."

With that answer, he burst out laughing. He carried on boisterously, cynically, insultingly. I waited calmly.

"You fool," he began again in another tirade of anger—"you prate about God. Not you nor God nor anything can stop me. I get what I go after, and I get it regardless. No one has ever stopped me yet." His arrogance seemed to have no limit, and he revealed himself—mind and body—but the victim of his emotions. His reason was unable to function, as is always the case under any uncontrolled feeling—or it would have warned him to go no further—with his insults.

I felt the expansion of the God-Power—again. 'This time it came stronger and stronger—until in a tone like a clarion, the Mighty Inner-Voice of my God-Self revealed the Truth of the whole transaction—and the deception at the mine.

"Mrs. Atherton," I said, "there has been gross deceit practiced upon you. Your workmen made a rich strike. This man had a spy among them who has bribed your superintendent—to remain silent concerning it." The superintendent and the others in the room went white and speechless, as my Inner-Self continued to expose their treachery. The prospective buyer seemed equal to any emergency, and interrupting me in his wild anger, shouted:

"You lie. I'll brain you for such interference." He lifted his steel cane and as I raised my hand to seize it—a White Flame suddenly shot forth flashing—

full in his face. He dropped to the floor as if struck by lightning. Then My Mighty God-Self spoke again with All Authority of Eternity, Majestic, Powerful:

"Let no one in this room move—until given permission." My outer self no longer me—but "God in Action"—stepped to where the man lay, and went on:

"Great Soul in this man—I speak to you! Too long have you been held prisoner—by his dominating personal self. Come forth—now! Take command of his mind and body! Right the many deceptions he has practiced—in the present life. Within the hour—this strong outer human creation of discord and injustice—which he has built up shall be consumed—and never again—shall it deceive or humanly dominate—another of God's children. To the outer self, I say—Awaken! In peace, love, kindliness, generosity and good will to all that lives."

Slowly, the color began to come back into the man's face, and he opened his eyes in strange bewilderment. "God in me"—still in charge, took him gently by the hand and putting an arm under his shoulder helped him to a large easy chair. Again, It commanded:

"My Brother—look at me!"

As he raised his eyes to mine, a tremor passed over his body, and in a voice scarcely audible said:

"Yes, I have seen. I understand—how wrong I have been. God forgive me." He dropped his head in his hands and hid his face—silent and ashamed. Tears began to drop through his fingers and he wept like a child.

"You will pay this dear lady, one million dollars," My God-Self continued, "and give her a ten per cent interest in the mine beside—for in the strike recently made is at least—ten million in gold ore." With deep humility and a strange sweetness, he answered:

"Let it be done now." He requested his men this time, instead of ordering them as was his former habit, to draw up the papers—as had been directed. Mrs. Atherton and he both signed—completing the transaction.

I turned to the others in the room, and realized from the expression on their faces all of them had been so lifted in consciousness—they had seen beyond the human veil—each of them saying:

"Never, so help me God, will I ever attempt to deceive or do wrong to my fellow man again." They had been raised to fully recognize and accept the God-Self within—every one.

It was late afternoon, when this occurrence took place. Mrs. Atherton extended a cordial invitation to remain as her guests over night, and accompany her to Phoenix in the morning—for the recording of the papers for the sale. After dinner that night, we gathered in the big living room before a large open fire-place. Everyone sincerely sought more understanding of the—Great Cosmic Laws of Life.

They asked—how it happened I had come into this kind of knowledge, and I told them of the Master Saint Germain and the way I had met him. I related some of my experiences on Mount Shasta, and how in the course of our conversation in regard—to the Great Cosmic Law—he had said:

"My Son, the Great Cosmic Law does not discriminate any more than does the multiplication table, if one makes a mistake in its application—or electricity, when one, who is ignorant of the—Law—governing its use, tries to direct its force—without knowledge of the way to control it.

"The Great Immutable Decrees—which forever keep order in the Infinite Realm of manifested Life—are all based upon the 'One Great Principle of Creation'—LOVE. That is the Heart—the Source of All, and the very Hub upon which—existence in form takes place.

"Love is Harmony—and without it in the beginning of a form—that form could not come into existence at all. Love is the co-hesive Power of the Universe, and without it—a Universe could not be.

"In your scientific world, Love expresses itself, as the attractive force between the electrons. It is the directive Intelligence which Wills them into form—the Power which keeps them whirling around a central core—and the Breath within the core—that draws them to it. The same thing is true of each vortex of force—everywhere in creation.

"A central core and the electrons whirling around it form an atom. This core of Love is to the atom—what the magnetic pole is to the earth—and what the spine is to the human body. Without a central core or Heart Center—there is only the unformed—Universal Light—the electrons filling Infinity and whirling around the—Great Central Sun.

"The electron is Pure Spirit or 'Light' of God. It remains forever Uncontaminated and Perfect. It is—Eternally Self-sustained, Indestructible, Self-luminous and Intelligent. If it were not, it could not and would not obey 'The Law'—the directing activity of Love. It is Immortal, Ever-Pure, Intelligent Light-Energy, and the only Real True Substance out of which everything in the Universe is made—The Eternally Perfect 'Life-Essence' of God.

"Inter-stellar space is filled with this pure 'Light-Essence.' It is not dark and in chaos, as has been the ignorant, limited concept of puny human intellects. This Great Sea of Universal Light—that exists everywhere throughout Infinity—is constantly being drawn into form, and given a quality of one kind or another, according to the way the electrons are held around a central point or core by—Love.

"The number—of electrons which combine with each other—in a specific atom—is the result of and determined by—conscious thought. The rate—at which they whirl around the central core—is the result of and determined by—feeling. The intensity—of the drawing and whirling motion within the central core is the—'Breath of God' and therefore, the most—Concentrated Activity of Divine Love. Speaking in scientific terms it would be called—centripetal force. These are the determining factors—which make the quality—of an atom.

"Thus, you will see the atom is an entity—a living, breathing thing—created or brought into existence by the—Breath and Love of God—through the—Will of Self-Conscious Intelligence. In this way, the 'Word is made flesh.' The machinery—that Self-Conscious Intelligence uses to accomplish this manifestation of its Being—is thought and feeling.

"Destructive thought and discordant feeling so rearrange the ratio and rate of speed of the electrons—within the atom—that the duration of the Breath of God—within the pole—is changed. The duration of the Breath—is decreed by the Will of the Consciousness—using that particular kind of atom. If that Conscious Directing Will is withdrawn—the electrons lose their polarity—and fly apart seeking their way back—Intelligently mind you—to the 'Great Central Sun' re-polarizing themselves. There they receive Love only—the Breath of God is never-ending—and Order—the First Law—is Eternally maintained.

"Some scientists have claimed and taught that planets collide in space. No such thing is possible. To do so—would be to throw the entire scheme of Creation into chaos. It really is fortunate indeed—that the 'Mighty Laws of God' are not limited—to the opinions—of some of the children of earth. It does not matter what any scientist—mundane or otherwise thinks—God-Creation—is ever moving forward—and expressing more and more—Perfection.

"The constructive thought and harmonious feeling within a human mind and body are the Activities of Love and Order. These permit—the Perfect Ratio and Speed of the electrons within the atom to remain permanent, and thus, they stay polarized at their particular point in the Universe, as long as the duration of the—Breath of God—within their core—is held steady by the Will—of the Directing Self-Conscious Intelligence using the body in which they exist. In this way, the quality of Perfection and the maintenance of Life in a human body is—always—under the conscious control of the Will of the individual occupying it. The Will of the Individual is Supreme—over his temple—and even in cases of accident—no one leaves his body-temple—until he wills to do so. Very often pain in the body, fear, uncertainty, and many other things influence the personality to change its decisions concerning what it has willed in the past—but everything that happens to the body—is and will always be—under the control of the individual's free will.

"To understand the above explanation—concerning the electron and the conscious control the individual has—through his thought and feeling—to govern the atomic structure of his own body—is to understand the—One

Principle Governing—form throughout Infinity. When man will make the effort to prove this to himself—or within his own atomic flesh-body—he will then proceed to Master Himself. When he has done—that—all else in the Universe is his—willing co-worker—to accomplish whatsoever he wills—through Love.

"Whoever makes himself—willingly obedient—unto the 'Law of Love,' has—Perfection in his mind and world—Permanently maintained. Unto him and him alone does—All Authority and Mastery—belong. He—Only—has the right to Rule because he has first learned—to obey. When he has—obtained obedience—from the atomic structure within his own mind and body—all atomic structure outside of his mind and body will—obey him also.

"Thus, mankind through thought and feeling has the power—each individual Within himself—to rise to the Highest or sink to the lowest. Each one alone—determines his own pathway—of experience. By conscious control of his attention—as to what he allows his mind to accept—he can walk and talk with God—Face to Face—or looking away from God, become lower than the animals, sinking his human consciousness into—oblivion. In the latter case—the God-Flame Within him—then withdraws from its human habitation. After aeons of time, it tries a human journey once again—into the world of physical matter, until—final victory—is accomplished consciously—and of its own Free-Will."

"I told them of the limitless possibilities which Saint Germain had shown me were before mankind for accomplishment, whenever they are willing to accept The Great God—'Presence Within' every Individual—as the directing and accomplishing power. The buyer of the mine asked me why I used the word—acceptance—so often, and I recalled the words Saint Germain had used in explaining it to me, for he said:

"Even in the outer activity of your Life, if you purchase a thing or are offered something marvelous and perfect, if you do not—accept—it, it would be impossible for you to use—or have the benefit from it. So it is—with the 'Great God-Presence' Within us. Unless, we—accept—that our Life is God-Life—and that all power and energy we have with which to do anything is God-Power—and God-Energy—how can we have—GOD-Qualities and accomplishment—in our world?

"As Sons of God, we are commanded to choose—whom we shall serve, the Mighty 'Presence' of God Within us—or the outer human self. The gratification of the outer human appetites and sense demands—has one and only one result—misery, degradation, and destruction.

"All Constructive Desire is really the God-Self Within—pushing Perfection forward—into the use and enjoyment of the outer self. The Great Energy of Life—is flowing through us constantly. If we direct It to constructive accomplishment—It brings joy and happiness. If directed to sense gratification, there cannot be anything but misery as a result because it is all the action of—Law—an Impersonal Life-Energy.

"Keep before the outer activity of your mind the constant reminder that you are 'Life'—'God in Action' in you and your world. The personal self is continually claiming things and power of its own—when the very Energy by which it exists—is loaned it—by the God-Self. The outer personal human activity does not even own—its skin. The very atoms of its body are loaned to it—by the 'Supreme God-Presence' from the Great Sea of Universal Substance.

"Train yourself to return all power and authority to the 'Great Glorious God-Flame' which is your 'Real Self' and the 'Source' from which you have always received every good thing." We talked until two o'clock in the morning, and then, I had to suggest—we retire. No one wanted to sleep but I said to them:

"You will sleep in the arms of God," and the next morning, they were surprised to realize how quickly they had dropped off to sleep.

We were up at seven, and on our way to Phoenix. The recording was completed, and I explained I must leave—as my work with them was finished for the time being. They were all deeply grateful and anxious to know more. I promised to keep in touch with them and give further help, as the Master Saint Germain should direct. As I was leaving the buyer of the mine turned to me, and said:

"I don't care what anyone thinks of me—I want to embrace you—and thank you from the bottom of my heart—for saving me from the ruin of my outer self—and for revealing the 'Great Light.' I bowed my head in deep humility, and replied:

"Thank God—I am but the channel. God alone is the Great 'Presence' and Power—that does all things well." Mrs Atherton turned to me and expressed her feeling:

"I do praise and thank the God in you—for the Mighty Protecting 'Presence,' and never in my Life shall I cease to thank God and you—for the—Light—this experience has brought us all.

"I feel certain we shall all meet again," I replied and bidding everyone, good-bye, turned my face once more toward Mount Shasta—arriving at my lodge the evening of the second day.

Two weeks later, I felt a strong impulse to make one more trip to my trysting place—with the Master Saint Germain. I started at four in the morning, and reached the edge of the dense timber about nine.

The plaintive cry of my panther friend came to my ears—before I had gone twenty paces into the woods. I answered quickly. In a moment he came bounding to my side with all the welcome of an old time friend, and we proceeded onward to our meeting-place.

I noticed the panther was very restless, and acted as if laboring under some inner agitation. This was most unusual—for he had always been very quiet, when in my presence. I patted and stroked the beautiful head but it made—no difference. I sat down and we ate lunch.

"Come on old boy," I said as we finished, "let's go for a walk." He gave me a long steady look, the most pathetic expression I have ever seen. I could not understand it.

We had gone some distance, when we came to a cliff about fifteen feet high at the top of which—hung a projecting rock. Something caused me to look at the panther. The expression in his eyes was wild and fierce. I sensed a sort of tension in the atmosphere but did not realize—what it was. I walked on a few paces farther, and felt a—chill pass over me. Looking up suddenly, I saw a mountain lion crouched—ready to spring. The next instant—it leaped toward me. I threw myself against the cliff—and the lion landed beyond—where I had stood. Like a flash of lightning—the panther sprang and the two locked in mortal combat.

No words can describe the terror of the struggle—that followed. They screamed, rolled, tore, and clawed each other. The lion was considerably heavier, and it seemed for a time, as if it would gain the advantage. However, the panther was the faster moving of the two, and finally broke away. There was just an instant's pause until it saw a chance, and then with one spring landed on the lion's back, and fastened its teeth—just behind the ears.

The panther's grip was like steel, and after a few seconds of rolling and twisting, the lion's struggles grew weaker. Finally they ceased altogether. The panther came reeling toward me—his side terribly torn. He looked up at me all the fierceness gone from his eyes—and his energy ebbing fast. There passed an expression of contentment over the face, and suddenly—giving a plaintive cry—he fell over dead at my feet.

I stood motionless, and wept silently at the loss of my friend—for I had become almost as attached to him as to a human companion. The next instant, I looked up, and beside me stood—Saint Germain.

"My Beloved Brother, be not sad or dismayed," he said, "your contact with the panther had so quickened its consciousness—that it could no longer remain in that present body, and the Great Cosmic Law—demanded from it some service—to you. This it gave in love by saving your life. All is truly well." He touched the thumb of his right hand to my forehead.

"Be at peace," he continued, as the feeling of grief left me, and I felt completely relieved. "The Great Cosmic Law is unerring. We cannot receive without giving, and we cannot give without receiving. Thus, the Great Balance of Life is maintained.

"I congratulate you sincerely on the service rendered at the mine, and your serenity during the occurrence. All concerned with that transaction—will—become great helpers to humanity.

"Soon, you will be called upon to render a far greater service—than any you have given so far. In it, remember always it is God's Power and Intelligence acting, and your mind and body—only the channel. Until you meet with this experience, meditate constantly upon the 'Limitless Power of God' which can express through you at—any time."

I asked him what the Ascended Master's attitude is in regard to the many channels through whom partial Truth is given forth, and he replied:

"There are many sincere channels. Some have more understanding than others. All are God's children serving to the best of their ability with the understanding they have at present. We may not judge anyone—but we must—know and see only God—expressing in all. Our endeavor is to bless all activity—wherever it is. We see the 'Inner-Light' radiating through such activities, and this makes it impossible for us to be mistaken—as to whether they—are or are not—giving forth Truth.

"It is the same with individuals. Those—who offer their service in the Name of the Ascended Jesus Christ—will always receive more—than ordinary sustaining power." We had walked some distance, when he said:

"Come, I will accompany you home. Place your arm about my shoulder." I did so and felt my body lifted from the ground. In a few moments more, I was in my room at the lodge with Saint Germain standing beside me—smiling at my surprise.

"Meet me in seven days," he said, "at our appointed place for then—we will finish our work in this part of the country." He smiled, bowed graciously, and slowly faded from sight. The last thing that remained visible—as he gradually disappeared—were his marvelous, beautiful eyes—smiling back at me.

As I meditated each day upon the "Great God-Presence Within," for my coming service, I realized more and more—how important it is—to keep the attention focused upon "That Presence Only"—no matter what appearances seem to indicate—in order to keep any outer condition—from affecting me. In one of Saint Germain's conversations, he had stressed particularly the all importance of keeping my outer self harmonious, and in regard to this had said:

"My Son, you cannot realize—how very great is the necessity—for harmony in the outer self—if the Fulness of the Inner Perfection and Power—is to be expressed—in your outer life. The importance of keeping a Feeling of peace, love, and serenity in the—personal self—cannot be emphasized too strongly—for when this is done the "Mighty God-Presence Within" can act—without limit—in an instant.

"The continual Outpouring of a Feeling of Peace and Divine Love to every person and everything unconditionally—no matter whether you think it be deserved or not—is the Magic Key—that unlocks the door and—releases instantly—this 'Tremendous Inner God-Power.' Fortunate indeed is—he—who has learned this 'Law' for—he then seeks to—BE—All Peace and Love. Without It—humanity has nothing good, and—with It—they have all things 'Perfect.' Harmony is the Keynote—the 'One Great Law of Life.' Upon It rests—All Perfect Manifestation—and without It all form disintegrates and returns into the Great Sea of Universal Light."

The following seven days, I spent much time in meditation. I felt a greater and greater peace growing within me—until by the sixth day, it seemed as if my entire consciousness were like a great calm sea.

On the morning of the seventh day, I left my lodge at four o'clock and reached our meeting place at ten thirty. I sat down on a log to wait with a feeling of wonderful exhilaration—which I knew to be the result of my meditation. I was so deep within the contemplation of my God Self—I did not hear anyone approaching—until a voice spoke to me.

I looked up, and saw an old man with white hair and beard, whom I thought at first sight, was an old prospector, although his clothing was too clean for that occupation. As he came up to me and held out his hand, that too confirmed my feeling—he was not a laboring man. We exchanged greetings, chatted for a few moments on generalities, then he turned to me, and said:

"My Friend, I would like to tell you a story. It won't take long. I haven't told it to anyone for a long time. I would like to try once more.

By that time I began to have a feeling of intense interest. It occurred to me he might be thirsty, and as I reached for a cup to get him a drink—from the spring by which we stood—a crystal cup formed within my hand—like the one Saint Germain had held out to me several times. The old man looked up and with eyes shining and excited, almost shouted:

"It is he! It is he!"

I did not know what to do, so I insisted—he drink. As I looked within the cup, I saw it was filled with the same clear—Sparkling Liquid—the Master had given me. The old man grasped it eagerly, and—with an intense expression of the deepest gratitude I have ever seen—drank the contents. He immediately became very calm and quiet—but with it all a deep, intense sincerity. I asked him again to tell me the story, and he began by saying:

"My father was a British officer stationed in the Punjab of India where we made our home. When I was sixteen, he financed a friend who went to South Africa—to try his luck in the diamond mines, but my father never heard from him afterward.

"The year I was twenty, a tall handsome stranger, a man of great wisdom, visited my father at our home. He had come to bring a message from father's friend.

"'I bring you news,' he explained, 'from the friend whom you financed four years ago. He met with great success on that venture—in fact became very wealthy. He has recently passed on at the mines, and left no relatives. His entire fortune has been left to you and in case of your passing—it is to go to your son. If you desire, I will take charge of the matter and have it transferred—at once.'

"'I cannot leave India at the present time,' my father replied, 'for I am on government duty here. I appreciate greatly your offer to take care of the matter for me.' I was standing nearby during their conversation, and when they had completed arrangements the stranger turned to me.

"'My son,' he said, 'when you find the man who will offer you a—crystal cup of Sparkling Liquid—you will have met the one—who can assist you in raising the body. I cannot tell you more than this, except that you will find him—on a great mountain in North America. This may seem vague to you now but—it is all I can say.'

"The stranger left, and a month later my father, who had ridden out to adjust certain government matters with the natives, was shot, and passed on before he could be brought home. I was an only son, and after another month, mother and I prepared for our return to England. Just before we left the same stranger came again, and said he was ready to transfer father's fortune to me. I explained, father had been shot.

"'Yes,' the stranger replied, 'when I left two months ago, I knew your father would pass on before my return. I have arranged for the fortune to be transferred to you, or rather to the Bank of England—for you. Here is money you may wish to use on the journey home, also the papers of transfer, and the credentials you will need at the bank. Present them, and you will receive custody of your wealth. Much of it is in diamonds of the first quality.' I thanked him, and offered to pay for his services and kindness but he replied:

"'Your kind intent is greatly appreciated but that is—already adjusted. I will be happy to accompany you to the steamer at Bombay.'

"The trip revealed to me his great wisdom and beside him—I felt like an infant. I know now—he enveloped me in a Radiation which has stayed with me—throughout the years. He arranged for transportation, accompanied us to the boat, and his last words to me were:

"'Remember—the "Crystal Cup." Seek and you shall find.'

"After a most wonderful voyage, we arrived at Southampton—went on to London, and presented my credentials to the Bank of England. The official to whom I presented them remarked:

"'Yes, we were expecting you today. Here are your bank and checking books.'

"I looked at them to see how much my fortune amounted to and was amazed to learn—a hundred thousand pounds—had been placed to my credit. Five years later, my mother passed on. I transferred one half of my wealth to a bank in New York and began the search for 'the man with the Crystal Cup.'

"I can never repeat the disappointments, the trials, the sorrow I have been through but in the face of everything, somehow—I could never give up. The thing which seems so strange to me is—while I have grown old in outer appearance, my energy and strength are as great as ever—sometimes I think greater—than in my fullest youth.

"In years, I am seventy. Today, I just wanted to follow this trail, and praise God I have found you. My desire was so great—it was almost irresistible."

"But my good man," I asked, "what am I to do for you?"

"You will know," he replied, "for I know I have made no mistake. In the heart of this majestic mountain is a Great Power. I feel it. Ask God—to show you what to do."

Suddenly, I felt the "Mighty God-Power" surging forth so strong—it almost lifted me from the ground. Making the sign—Saint Germain had taught me, I called to God for "Light" and raising my hand in salutation said:

"Mighty God in man and the Universe! We seek Thy Light! We seek Thy Wisdom! We seek Thy Power! Let Thy Will be done in and for this, My Brother, who has sought and found me to do for him—I know not what. Thou knowest! Manifest Thy Will through my mind and body, and let what ever is to be done for this Brother—Thy Son—come forth."

As my hand came down, it held the—Crystal Cup—filled with "Living Liquid-Light." I offered it to him, and my—Mighty God-Self spoke—again.

"Drink without fear. Thy search is ended."

He drank the contents without a moment's hesitation. I stepped forward quickly—and took both his hands in mine. Slowly and steadily—every vestige of age—disappeared from him, and the God in me continued:

"Behold! Thou art forever Free from all earthly limitation. Ascend now—unto the 'Ascended Host of Light'—who await Thee."

Very slowly, he began to rise from the ground, and as he did so, his human garments disappeared, and he became clothed in raiment of Glistening White. I let go his hands. Then in a voice of deepest Love, he said:

"I shall return to thee—Beloved Brother. Well shalt thou be repaid for this—Transcendent Service. Thou wert the—only one—through whom—this—could be done for me. Some day, thou shalt see why," and with a happy smile, he disappeared on—a Radiant Pathway of "Light."

As the Mighty God-Power Within me receded, I was so astounded—I fell on my knees and offered the deepest prayer of my Life in grateful humility and praise for the—privilege—of giving such service.

I rose and the Master Saint Germain received me into his wondrous embrace.

"My Beloved Brother!" he said, "I am greatly pleased. Noble and faithful was your attendance upon the Great God Within you. Beautifully did you receive your Mighty 'God in Action.' I do indeed congratulate you. You will ever be held within Our Embrace, even though outwardly you may not always be aware of it.

"You have become a worthy 'Messenger' of the Great White Brotherhood and the Ascended Host. Hold close to your—Mighty God Self. Thus, you will ever be ready for service—wherever and for whatever—is required. My Love enfolds you—until we meet again. I will keep you informed."

Slowly, I wended my way back to the lodge, every step praise and gratitude to the "One Mighty God" that molds us all into "Eternal Perfection."

CHAPTER - IX

Venus Visits the Royal Teton

ANY weeks had passed, and the morning of December, thirty-first, nineteen hundred thirty, came and with it—the Master, Saint Germain.

"Be ready at seven o'clock tonight," he instructed, "and I will call for you. Focus your attention as much as possible on the—Glory of God Within yourself—that you may receive the full benefit intended—on this Divine Occasion. Remember your Twin Ray and son—for the three of you will be honored guests—of the Brotherhood of the Royal Teton—at their New Year Assembly tonight."

I spent the remainder of the day in deep meditation. He arrived at seven o'clock and as I had already placed my physical body in bed—I stepped forth—in the one he had prepared for me.

"Tonight," he continued, "an experiment is to be tried—which has not been accomplished—for over seventy thousand years. We feel perfectly confident of success on this occasion, as all are now well prepared. Come."

We must have travelled at great speed, although I did not realize it, and soon stood on the apex of the Royal Teton, where the heavy covering of snow made it glisten in the moonlight like millions of diamonds. As we approached the entrance to the tube, I noticed a clearing around it for a radius of at least a hundred feet. As we stepped within it, the atmosphere felt warm and comfortable. We passed on through the entrance—which had been opened for those attending the New Year celebration.

Saint Germain and I entered the great audience chamber, and met Lotus and our son—who had already arrived with their escort—Amen Bey. Our joy on this occasion was very great—for we had not been together on the physical plane for some two years, and during that time, while working out of the body, each had been occupied with his own individual activities—which necessitated our being in different channels at the Inner levels.

The great room was brilliantly lighted, and the glorious fragrance of roses and lotus blossoms filled the air. The sweetest, most delightful music floated in from everywhere. Many had already come and others were arriving every few moments.

We noticed a large object—covered with a golden cloth—had been placed in the center of the room—but as no explanation was offered concerning it, we remained silent. Saint Germain presented us to the guests, and then led the way into a room filled with rare musical instruments. We saw a great pipe organ and four harps made of a substance like pearl with posts of gold, the sounding boards and upper parts being constructed of white metal. The high strings on the harps were silver wound, the bass ones gold and—the material of which they were made—gave forth a tone—that combined the sounds produced by metal, wood and the human voice. The tone of these instruments can only be known by being heard, for they were different from anything which has ever been used in the outer world of music in the West. The sound—produced by this unusual material—more nearly resembles some of the wonderful tones of the esraj, an instrument used in India.

We saw four violins—also made of a substance that looked like pearl—but the resonance is far beyond that—of any known wood. The strings were wound with both gold and silver and produced a beauty of tone almost beyond description. We heard all these instruments—played later that evening.

Returning to the Great Audience Hall, Saint Germain showed Lotus and our son—the beautiful portraits—which had been recently transferred from the temple of Mitla in Oaxaca, Mexico. He escorted them through the record room—where they were shown the evidence—of my former observations with him.

For the work being done during this New Year celebration, all members of the Royal Teton were clothed—in plain golden robes of gorgeous material—with the emblem of the Brotherhood on the left breast—embroidered so it looked like dark blue velvet, the same shade as the great panel—that formed—the Cosmic Mirror.

There were seventy men, thirty-five ladies, and—the Presiding Master, Lanto—who is the Blessed Brother—in charge of this Retreat. When all had assembled who belonged to this branch, he stepped forward and addressed them saying:

"It is now eleven o'clock and time for our meditation. Tonight, let us pour out adoration unto the 'Great Light,' feel at 'One' with our own—Divinity—for thirty minutes, and during the following thirty minutes know the 'Oneness' of Venus with our earth. All take their accustomed stations, and form an elliptic in the center of the room."

For one hour, it seemed as though a hundred and six golden figures were united in one breath—so completely were they in unison. At the close of the meditation—a joyous burst of music filled the immense hall, and—Lanto stepped before—the Great Mirror.

He extended his hands and—a Tremendous Blaze of "Light"—flashed forth upon it, revealing a group of people—far in the distance—surrounded by golden, rose, and violet "Light," Dazzling in its Beauty and Radiance.

They drew nearer, and the same glorious, wondrous colors filled the great audience chamber—giving everyone a tremendous feeling of uplift and power.

Presently, Twelve Guests from Venus—stood in our midst—robed in White, Scintillating Garments—surpassing all power of description. There were seven gentlemen and five ladies—all extremely handsome.

Six of the men were at least six feet four inches in height—the seventh fully two inches taller than the rest. The ladies were about five feet ten. All had light brown hair with the exception of the Tall Master and his was—a glorious pure gold. Their brilliant, piercing, violet-blue eyes were beautiful and fascinating.

The Tall Master gave the salutation of the East, touching his heart and forehead with the finger tips of his right hand—and bowed low—before Lanto. The others also came forward, greeted him, and were presented to those assembled. Lanto gave a brief address of welcome, only the following part of which is permitted to be recorded:

"In the 'Presence' of the One Supreme God—and those of the 'Great White Brotherhood' assembled here—these Twelve Guests from Venus are made 'Members of the Brotherhood of the Royal Teton.'"

The Tall Master was made Presiding Master for the evening. He acknowledged the welcome, stepped to the center of the room, and caused the golden cloth to be removed from the objects it covered.

Lo! before us stood—the three crystal caskets—still containing the sustained bodies of Lotus, our son, and myself. They looked—as if the forms had just gone to sleep, glowing with perfect health. The Presiding Master turned to us and said:

"Are you ready?" and we three answered, in the affirmative.

"Then, take your places by the containers," he directed.

We obeyed and immediately—a Marvelous Radiance gathered and drew close around the bodies and ourselves—the intensity increasing rapidly—until we must have been invisible to the outer sight. In a few moments—the Radiance diminished—and to our amazement—the caskets were empty. We stood there—clothed in those bodies we had laid aside so long ago—which had been sustained and purified by the "Flame of Life"—during these many centuries.

The transformation was amazing and—the feeling cannot be described—for we were as much surprised—as is the reader. However, the human side of anyone, even at its best, knows so little of the Tremendous Wonders—existing everywhere around us all the time, and the Infinite Possibilities within every plane of Life—that all things are possible, and—the closer we live—in Love and recognition of our Divinity, the more of these Wonders throughout Creation—will be revealed in our individual lives.

The experiment had proved a success and, as we moved about among the Brothers and Sisters, all congratulated the Master and ourselves upon the accomplishment. They greatly rejoiced that—so strange an experiment had become a mighty Truth—many commenting upon how much those bodies resembled the ones of the Visitors from Venus.

The crystal caskets were then removed to their room, and the wonderful musical instruments—brought into the audience chamber. Saint Germain played the first number on the great organ, a composition he called "Hearts Of The Future." It seemed to me the most delicate, colorful, yet powerful music that ever came from an organ on earth. While he played—the most beautiful colors—gorgeous past description—poured through the atmosphere of the enormous room.

A group played the next number. The Master Saint Germain at the organ, three of the Lady Masters from Venus, and Lotus played four harps, two of the Brothers from Venus, our son, and I played four violins. When all were in readiness the words—"Souls In Ecstacy"—flashed out above the organ, as Saint Germain played the prelude. All entered deeply into the fulness and joy of that marvelous music. The Volume and Power swelled into such Magnitude—it seemed as though the Beauty and Glory of that Joy must send forth enough God-Consciousness—to lift all mankind—yes—even the earth itself—into Everlasting Perfection.

There were four more numbers—played with the same Tremendous Power to lift and harmonize everywhere—until we felt as if—the very mountain would float away. At the close of the music, the instruments were returned to their room, and the Presiding Master seated all in proper order—before the Great Mirror. He took his place at the point of earth's triangle—and scenes of wonder from Venus—began to appear—he—explaining every detail that did not explain itself.

The pictures revealed much of their system of education—showing astronomical instruments—whose perfection would make the scientific world of today speechless—with admiration and astonishment—and geologist's equipment for examining the interior of the stratas of the planets—of both Venus and earth. We saw inventors and several of their tremendous discoveries—surpassing our fondest imagination.

"Many of these inventions," explained the Master, "will come into use on earth in—the Golden Crystal Age—we have now entered."

Some of the principal inventions—that are to be utilized on earth—were explained and could humanity have seen them—it would take heart and be tremendously encouraged—in regard to the future. It may be these pictures from Venus—will be taken up and described in a separate work later—providing permission can be obtained.

The scenes from Venus finished, and those concerning the earth came on the screen. Many changes were shown to take place in the next seventy years.

These affected Europe, Asia, India, North and South America, and revealed to us—that regardless of all appearances at the present time—the sinister force attempting to create chaos and destruction throughout the world—will be completely destroyed. When that is accomplished—the mass of humanity—will turn to the "Great God Presence" within each heart and also governing the Universe. "Peace Shall Reign On Earth—and Man Send Out Good Will To Man." This Revelation was stupendous. The closing scenes followed next—and these concerned principally the United States in the next century. The progress and advancement she will make is almost—unbelievable.

These things are true for the "Great God Law" makes no mistakes and—the Revelations of that New Year's night—are God's Eternally True Records.

Certain great souls were shown who would awaken, be Raised, and added to the—Host of Ascended Ones—to carry forward this great progress. The Presiding Master—then reminded those present—of the "Blessed Kumaras" and in a voice filled with Love and Adoration gave the following explanation—in tribute to them.

"The Seven Kumaras, whom some Inner students have known as—'Lords of The Flame' from Venus—were the Only Ones from this entire system of planets—who of their own free will and infinite Love—offered to guard the children of earth and assist their upward progress. They came and gave Transcendent Help here—at the most critical period of earth's growth. It was the time of initiation that is most dangerous in the Life of a planet and its humanity, but through their protection and guidance, the goal was attained—and mankind has been enabled to reach—the 'Greater Heights.'

"Many of the Brothers understand—that every twenty five hundred years—the Kumaras release a greatly increased Outpouring of Cosmic Love—Wisdom—and Energy. This Blazing Light and Transcendent Radiance—flooding the earth and its inhabitants—interpenetrating all—is a Tremendous Lifting Process, and gives a forward impulse to the growth of the entire earth, as well as its humanity.

"Just preceding each of these Great Outpourings extraordinary physical disturbances occur, and general unrest is felt throughout—by the people. Such disturbance is due to the discord that has accumulated during the last—of the preceding period. The generation of such inharmony is due—always—to the wandering away from the fundamental 'Principle of Life'—and the human sense disturbance thus created—pollutes the outer activity of mankind, the earth, and its atmosphere.

"It is to cleanse this, and bring humanity back to—the Original Purity of Life—that cataclysmic action takes place. It is following these periods, the Kumaras release an Enormous Outpouring of 'LIGHT'—to illumine and strengthen earth's children, ultimately enabling them to make—the Supreme Attainment.

"We are approaching another such period, and this time the release of the Great Cosmic Love, Wisdom and Energy—the Mighty Rays of Light—will not only quicken the minds of the race but the atomic structure of earth as well—making it more 'Luminous' in our solar system. Never, since these Great Lords of the Flame came to earth—have conditions permitted such a Great Outpouring to take place—as will occur ere long. Many—who have seemed to become hardened by their former activities, will awaken, as it were almost over night, and feel—the Nearness of the Great God 'Presence'—within each heart. Many, who have been meek and humble but holding close to the 'Inner Presence,' will suddenly blaze forth amazing themselves as well as others—by the Transcendent Light, they will manifest. All will be done by the Power of God-Love, and humanity will truly begin to realize—that it is the height of folly—for one part of God's Creation—to war against another part.

"The desire to bless others instead of themselves—will almost involuntarily—enter into the hearts of mankind, and send forth a 'Light'-that will illumine the rest of the 'Way to Perfection.'

"Selfishness alone—holds the children of this sphere in the bondage and misery—which have been allowed to express upon earth—but when the 'Light of the Christ' expands the 'Love in the Heart,' selfishness flees and returns to the sea of forgetfulness.

"Great, natural, physical changes will take place. Two Great Centers of 'Light'—will pour forth their blessing to humanity—one—the Glorious Glistening 'Presence' of Shamballa in its Dazzling Radiance—and the other—will appear in the United States—not however where any so far have been led to believe—but at a point—which has not yet been indicated to—outer channels—of the world.

"During the present activity of assistance and intense outpouring of 'Light' by the Great Ascended Host—who minister to the children of earth, hundreds of humanity—will find their present physical bodies—being quickened by the rapid raising—of the vibratory rate and, as this is completed will realize—that human, physical limitation and discord have dropped away like an old worn out garment, and that they—the Children of Light—stand forever at 'One' with the 'Flame of Life-Everlasting' and the 'Perfection of Eternal Youth and Beauty' a Visible Tangible Reality.

"Beloved children of earth, you stand upon the Threshold of the Ages. Its door is being held open by the 'Great Ones of Love' who ever invite you to walk consciously by their side in the—'Light.' No matter what the activities in the world without—walk with the 'Light' and in the 'Light'—regardless of appearances. Then, will you find a Master of the 'Light,' who has trod this self same path before you, ever watches and stands by your side revealing—the 'True Way.'

"The cycle changes—and we enter a New Dispensation—that brings with it a safer, more powerful, and yet rapid means by which the one climbing the

Path to Attainment is enabled to hold—Permanent Contact with the 'Great Cosmic Light.'

"In this New Order, the discipline for the neophyte—will be the focusing and maintaining—of his attention entirely—upon the three highest centers of the body, and he will do all his work at these points. Only the centers in the heart, throat, and head will receive conscious consideration and attention.

"The entire effort of the aspirant will be—to hold his attention upon these—for only by looking away from the lower centers—will he ever be able—to rise out of misery and limitation. The center at the top of the head is the highest focus in the human body, and there the Silver Cord of 'Liquid White Light' from the Great Source of Creation—enters.

"When the attention of the mind is held steadfast upon this, the Door of the Soul is opened and—the Three Fold Activity of the Pure White Light—encircles the waist just below the solar plexus—cutting off forever—the destructive activities of the animal nature in man. This permits his soul to leap forth into its Complete Divine Activity—united once more with the Perfection of Its Source—and Eternally thereafter—Master of all human creation—which means the discords of earth.

"Sincere students should meditate frequently upon the Perfect Action of the 'Golden Light' within the head—for It will illumine and teach the outer mind—all good things. This is the 'Light of the God Within.' One should feel It filling his entire consciousness—his body and world. This is the 'Light that lighteth every man that cometh into the world,' and there is no human being in existence—who has not some of this 'Light' within him.

"There are many throughout the earth—who are rapidly awakening, and feeling the Mighty Surge of this 'Inner Light' pouring itself out through them and thus—finding greater expression. If these will rigidly keep themselves harmonious—unflinchingly hold their attention upon the God Self Within—accept and visualize the Full Activity of Its Dazzling Radiance—they can encircle themselves in the Three-Fold Activity of the White Light. This cuts off—the discordant creation of the outer world.

"Beloved Brothers and Sisters, it will be our great joy and privilege to meet with you in January and July of each year, here in your Retreat because of—the Nearness and Outpouring of the All-controlling God-Light—which will soon be flooding America from shore to shore.

"Now, while the crystal containers are being brought in, let us meditate deeply upon the—'Oneness of Venus and the earth—the Omnipresence of Divinity—abiding in form.'"

We remained in deep silence for about ten minutes, and then the Presiding Master instructed us three—to take our places beside the caskets. He made the Sign of the heart and head, crossed his hands upon his chest, and called unto the "God-Presence":

"Thou Mighty Creator of the Universe and all it contains—Thou One Omnipresent God—we await the Manifestation of Thy Great Beneficent Presence."

A soft rose-colored "Luminous Essence" enveloped ourselves and the containers, drawing close about us. Suddenly—A Great Shaft of Dazzling White Light entered the enveloping Radiance—remained three or four minutes, and gradually faded from sight.

As we looked into the containers, the three bodies were resting within them. Observing each other, we were again clothed in the bodies—the Master, Saint Germain—had prepared for us—and because of which, we were enabled to visit the Great Assembly in the Royal Teton.

The Presiding Master blessed those assembled—the "Brotherhood of the Royal Teton" and all upon earth—promising to be with them again the following July.

The Twelve from Venus—then took their stations upon the circle in the floor of the audience hall.

The entire mountain trembled with the Mighty God Power—which they drew—and the "Light" thus focused took the form of an enormous eagle—its body violet and the head and feet of gold. The entire room became filled with a "Blazing White Light" forming one end of a "Great Pathway of Luminous Essence" on which the Twelve Radiant Beings returned to their home on Venus.

The Supreme Vision—those assembled gazed upon—surpasses anything words can describe. As the Great Vibratory Activity was lowered—a Wondrous Crystal Radiance illumined the Cosmic Mirror—and the words: "Peace and Illumination to all the earth and its inhabitants. Blessings from Venus"—appeared across its surface.

Each guest touched his heart and forehead, crossed his hands upon his chest and bowed in acceptance of—the Mighty Outpouring. All passed before Lanto, and received individual instruction for the work of nineteen thirty-one—then sat in deep silence and adoration unto the "Great Light." At the end of the meditation, a glorious burst of music filled the great hall and heads were bowed to receive His Blessing. His voice—clear, beautiful and resonant rang out:

"There is nothing Supreme but—God. There is nothing Eternal and Real but—The Christ. There is nothing True but—The Light. These Three are 'The One.' All else is shadow. Remember—shadows hide—shadows mislead—and shadows make mankind stumble.

"He, who walks the Pathway of Light—stands True to the Christ and looks always Godward, lives in a world of his own—untouched by the seething vortex about him—yet ever working in it, while the shadows last. These he turns his Light upon, and thus compels them to pass into the sea of forgetfulness.

"There is no happiness apart from facing and adoring the One Great God—The Source of All. There is nothing permanent but—Christ. There is no way to proceed through the Universe but on the 'Pathway of Light.'

"If you will arm yourselves with this Eternal Understanding of Life—swear allegiance only to your Source—God—stand True to the Christ—and carry the Light—you will accept as your code of honor the Obligation 'To Love and Bless Life'—no matter in what form it may be expressing, wherever you meet it.

"This is the Eternal Plan of Existence—and whosoever knows—That—may proceed anywhere in the Universe, explore all it contains, and yet be untouched by whatever shadows mankind has created, in its forgetfulness of—Whence It sprang.

"GOD alone is Great—and only unto 'The Source of All Greatness' does All Glory belong. He, who knows only his Source and refuses aught else is Wise indeed, for he becomes Permanent Happiness, and is—Master wherever he moves.

"Then and then alone—may he become Creator of Worlds. Upon these he bestows his happiness, and in this activity really lives the Divine Plan for All.

"Members of the Brotherhood of the Royal Teton—Reveal thou This Plan to the wayward children of earth. Shed Thy Radiance upon their self-created shadows, and point them 'The Way' to 'The Great Central Sun'—Our Transcendent Source. My Light enfolds you—My Power upholds you—and My Love breathes through you to those who seek their home in 'The Light.'

"Beloved Humanity—may this same Mighty Radiance shed its Light to illumine, heal, and bless you with That Divine Love which will ever hold All close in the Eternal Embrace of 'The One Supreme Light.'

"America—God bless you and clothe you—now—with the 'Everlasting Shadowless Light.'"

FINIS